THE BLUE BOOK OF STORIES

Tom Longano

RUNAWAY BOOKS

This is a work of fiction. Names, characters, events, and incidents are either the products of the author's imagination or used in a fictitious manner. Any resemblance to actual persons, living or dead, or actual events is purely coincidental.

For my students, with gratitude.

PRAISE FOR
THE BLUE BOOK OF STORIES

CONTENTS

1

THE BLUE BOOK OF STORIES

Mr L walked between the rows of desks in his fifth grade classroom, monitoring silent reading time. There was something odd today, something he couldn't quite place. No one fidgeted. Not a single hand went up to ask for the bathroom. No poorly disguised fart noise caused a storm of giggles. This was strange. This was actual silence.

Something must be wrong. Mr L examined each boy he passed, but all seemed to be reading quietly. Never in his years of teaching had he experienced such total silence during reading time. The all-boy elementary school had only three grades; third, fourth, and fifth, and Mr L had taught classes in each one. He'd even taught a class in the adjacent middle school. In his extensive experience as a teacher of young boys, there was nothing silent about 'silent reading time'. Instead, silent reading time was a perpetual battle between student and teacher, a battle that the teacher often lost.

But not today. Mr L returned to his desk and watched his students carefully. Leo sat closest to him, engaged in a large book with black and white pictures of World War I soldiers. Timmy, Leo's best friend and side-kick, had his nose an inch from a book on aquatic life. Porge, Jake, and Greg all read the same serial fantasy novel about wizards who become superstar athletes then turn into spies. Apparently, that was engrossing. Greg turned the pages so quickly he almost tore them off.

Charlie, Mr L's best student, had a copy of *Crime and Punishment* propped on his desk. Earlier, he'd asked Mr L about a recommended translation. Mr L made a mental note to check with Charlie's parents about this; there were certainly some themes in that book which might be considered inappropriate for a fifth grader.

Then Mr L stiffened. His gaze traveled to Albert, who was also reading a copy of *Crime and Punishment*. Albert was not Mr L's best student. He was not even close to the top five. Or ten. Mr L swiftly stood and walked over to Albert's desk. Albert shifted around, but Mr L couldn't see what he was doing until he reached him.

"Albert," he whispered, "what are you reading?"

"Just a book," said Albert quickly.

Mr L grabbed it. He turned some of the pages. It was *Crime and Punishment*.

"Interesting," he said. "What made you want to read this?"

"Charlie recommended it," Albert answered. "He said it had murder and stuff and I thought that was cool."

Mr L paused. Albert blinked up at him.

"Do you like it?" Mr L asked.

"It's alright, I guess."

Mr L glanced around the classroom. All the faces were turned toward him, watching. He realized that now he was disrupting their silent reading. Mr L returned the book to Albert's desk.

"Okay," he said. "Well, if you don't understand it, you can always try something else."

Albert nodded. Then he reopened the book and flipped to the page he was on. Mr L stared at him as if trying to solve a difficult puzzle. That's when he saw, out of the corner of his eye, Jeffrey.

Jeffrey was reading a colorful book with a prancing unicorn on the cover. This was not unusual for Jeffrey, but the book was upside-down.

Silently, Mr L slid round the desk and behind Jeffrey. Jeffrey was so captivated by his book that he didn't notice. Other boys did, though, and looked on with wide eyes. Leo cleared his throat, as if trying to warn Jeffrey. Jeffrey didn't hear. He turned another page, entranced.

Mr L leapt forward and snatched the book from his hand. To his surprise, another book fell out and onto the floor. It was small and fit behind the pages of the unicorn book. As Mr L stooped to pick it up, every boy in the class held his breath. Jeffrey trembled. Mr L examined the cover.

Dark blue, with golden lettering. *The Blue Book of Stories*. Mr L turned it over in his hands, confused.

"Jeffrey, what's this?" he said.

"Um," said Jeffrey, "a book, sir."

"What book?"

When Jeffrey didn't answer, Mr L looked away from the book to stare at him. The boy appeared earnest. Mr L wondered what sort of horrors could be in this book, that made it so secret, and so appealing to the likes of Jeffrey.

He glanced around the classroom. Sure enough, the same blue cover was sticking out of other books, or hastily crammed into desks, or hidden in laps. This was the reason for the silence. They were all reading the same book.

"Jeffrey, what is this book?" Mr L repeated.

"Sorry sir," Jeffrey stammered, "but, it's not for you."

"Not for me?"

"No sir."

"Well, who's it for then?"

Jeffrey didn't answer. Mr L tried again.

"What is this book?"

Jeffrey glanced around the classroom at the other boys. Then he looked back to the teacher and said:

"It's a book about my life, sir."

The bell rang to signify the end of silent reading. Mr L dismissed the class and they pushed out the door for break. Jeffrey held out his hands for his book, but Mr L did not give it back.

"I'm going to look at this a bit closer, Jeffrey," he said. "I'll return it to you after break."

Disappointed, Jeffrey joined the others outside the classroom. Mr L walked back to his desk. The fifth graders gathered at the window, sneaking glances to see if he was reading the book. Instead, he sat down and propped up their history text book, *Explorers and Visionaries of the Sixteenth Century*. His students lost interest, or pretended to, and meandered away. After a moment, Mr L snuck *The Blue Book of Stories* between the pages of his text book.

He was supposed to monitor their recess, but figured a few minutes reading wouldn't hurt. He needed to see what was in this strange book that Jeffrey and the other boys had tried to hide. He flipped through quickly; it appeared to be short stories. Then the names of the characters caught his eye. In fact, one character in particular. He glanced over his shoulder. Where in the world had they found this book?

Then Mr L could control himself no longer, he turned to the first chapter and began to read...

2

JEFFREY'S SPELLING TEST

Jeffrey hunched over his sheet of notebook paper, numbering each line. Mr L walked between the rows of desks and announced that the spelling test was about to begin. Jeffrey scribbled his name on the top of the page. He didn't have time for the date, he'd worry about that later. Every bit of his attention would be needed for spelling. His pencil tip quivered an inch from the page.

Mr L cleared his throat. The first word: "pineapple."

Nothing. Absolutely nothing. Jeffrey closed his eyes. He tried to breathe. He tried not to panic. His mind was blank.

Jeffrey had studied every night that week: two hours before dinner— one hour of copying the list, followed by another of flashcards— then a third hour after dinner— more flashcards— and finally, twenty minutes of his mom quizzing him in bed. Last night he couldn't sleep so he woke up and studied from two a.m. to four-thirty a.m., until his mom found out and confiscated his flashlight. All that studying led up to this moment. This was his chance to shine.

Mr L repeated the word: "pineapple."

Jeffrey panicked. It was his nerves, he knew it was his nerves, that's what his mom always said, 'don't lose your nerves, Jeffrey, don't get pressured, you're a smart boy but when you get pressured you forget everything.' Everything. Jeffrey felt pressured.

"Pineapple."

He inhaled deeply, then took a stab and wrote a G. This didn't seem right, so he erased it and wrote a B. That looked a bit better, so he followed it up with a quick R, T, and X. Then, remembering that every word needs at least one vowel, he tacked on an O.

"Okay," he said to himself, "'pineapple.'"

"Next word," said Mr L, "is 'dangerous.'"

Again, nothing. Jeffrey looked around in desperation. Other fifth graders scribbled down letters as if this was easy. Charlie already waited for the next word. Jeffrey looked back at his wrinkled sheet of paper.

"'Dangerous,'" Mr L repeated.

"Mr L?" Jeffrey's hand shot up.

"Yes, Jeffrey?"

"Um, could we, maybe, um, what's the first letter in 'dangerous'?"

The scribbling around him stopped. The other boys

exchanged glances. Mr L seemed to sigh.

"I mean, I know it," Jeffrey said quickly. "Like, I studied forever and I got 'dangerous' right like seven times, but I'm just blanking a bit and if I had the—"

"D," said Mr L, generously.

"Thank you sir, thanks so much."

Jeffrey grabbed the pencil and wrote a D. He raised his hand again.

"Yes, Jeffrey?"

"Hi, um, just wondering, well, maybe if we could all have the second letter—"

"No one wants the second letter," said Albert from the desk next to Jeffrey.

"Shut up," Jeffrey hissed back.

"I'm sorry, that's all I can give you," Mr L said. "We need to move on to the next word."

Jeffrey didn't hear the next word. Mr L had rounded a corner in the desks and Jeffrey leaned over to Albert. As much as he disliked Albert, he was desperate.

"Psst, Albert," he said, "Psssst—"

"I'm not giving you anything," said Albert shortly.

"I just need to know," Jeffrey whispered. "What's the second letter of 'dang—'"

"Z."

"Oh." Jeffrey paused. He hadn't expected Albert to be so helpful.

"You sure?"

"Yes."

"Nice."

Jeffrey wrote a Z. He couldn't help but chuckle to himself. This spelling test was becoming a piece of cake.

"Albert, Albert? Albert!"

"What?"

"What's the third letter in 'dang—'"

"Q."

"Nice."

Jeffrey wrote a Q. Then, per Albert's advice, he followed it with three more Z's and a backwards 4. Then he fist pumped. This test, this was a joke. Mr L was on the fourth word now: "limerick."

"Psst Albert—"

"The next person to talk without raising his hand will have his test taken away, and he will receive a zero."

There was a hush as the class snuck looks over to Jeffrey's desk. Mr L was looking right at him. Then he repeated, "'Limerick.'"

Jeffrey looked at his paper and tried to think of "limerick." Nothing. He looked at Albert, who now refused to look up. Jeffrey looked back to the paper. Still, nothing.

"Um, Mr L?"

"Jeffrey, I'm not taking questions now."

"But please, sir, I was just wondering if maybe we could have the first—"

"No, Jeffrey."

"I just, I studied, I just—"

"Put your hand down, Jeffrey."

"But I—"

"Write as much as you know."

"But—"

"Write it."

"B—"

"Now."

Mr L stood over Jeffrey's desk. Jeffrey's hand slowly descended. His fingers lifted the pencil. Shaking, he tried his best to write the first letter of "limerick": W. That didn't look right at all. He tried again: S. Jeffrey began to breathe very quickly. Mr L moved on to the next word, walking away.

"The next word is, 'kindergarten.'"

Then, out of the corner of his eye, Jeffrey saw that Charlie was not covering his paper. Charlie! Maybe the smartest fifth grader in the whole class. Actually, probably, Charlie was the smartest fifth grader in the whole world. And here he was, bleeding his test to Jeffrey. Jeffrey could hardly believe his good fortune. He realized he'd gotten "limerick" completely wrong! The first letter was K, followed by an I, then a N, then a D—

"Mr L, Jeffrey's looking at my paper," said Charlie.

"Not true!" Jeffrey snapped.

"You were hanging over my shoulder giggling like a weirdo!"

"Your face is a weirdo," said Jeffrey.

"Enough," said Mr L. "Charlie, Jeffrey, both of you get minus one for talking during the test. The next word is 'sanity.'"

The gasp that rippled through the classroom drowned

out Mr L's last sentence. Charlie turned bright red. He never got less than a hundred on a spelling test. Never. Now, with this minus one, the best grade he could get was a ninety-five.

Jeffrey snickered and elbowed Albert, lifting his eyebrows a couple times. Looks like old Charlie wasn't so smart after all. Albert glared at Jeffrey then put his head on his elbow so that his paper was completely hidden. Jeffrey frowned.

Mr L continued and each word sounded more and more like a foreign language. Jeffrey fought back panic with each breath. He couldn't do this again. He couldn't go home with another minus twenty. His mother would be devastated.

Then Jeffrey remembered his notecards. The corner of a single card was sticking out of his desk, right below his elbow. All he had to do was nudge it, just a little bit, and he would be able to see—

No. Jeffrey might've been a lot of things, but he was no cheater. He resolved to finish the spelling test on his own. He couldn't look at the answer. At least not now, because Mr L was standing right behind him.

Jeffrey paused. He had seen something new, something he could easily read without needing to turn his head. Miraculously, Albert's paper was being pushed inch by inch towards his desk. Every time Albert finished a word it came closer, so that Jeffrey could see what had been written before. He caught his breath. Albert turned, just the slightest bit of a turn, and winked.

Jeffrey felt an explosion of confidence. He was grateful for such good friends. Immediately he began to scribble down answers.

12. Iamapoop

13. Iamabigpoop

14. Ilikesmellysocks

15. Ismellpoopysocks

Jeffrey couldn't help but laugh. It was all too easy. How had he not noticed before that all the words started with an 'I'? This was such a piece of cake. He was going to get one hundred percent and his mom was going to put his test right on the fridge, so that everyone who came in the house would see it and ask about what a great, smart student Jeffrey was:

19. Ilickpoopsyum

Then, just in Jeffrey's moment of triumph, Albert flipped over his paper. Jeffrey froze. There was one more word. If he missed that, plus the minus one he already got from talking to Charlie, he would only have a ninety percent. That was not fridge material. He needed at least a ninety-five. Other students were flipping over their papers too. Mr L was repeating the final word: "adventurous." It was a long one. Jeffrey bit his pencil.

Then he saw the corner of the notecard. He realized that card must be word number twenty, because it was the last one he had studied and was on top of the stack. There it was, his almost perfect score. His hand twitched. Then he glanced up. And right into Mr L's eyes.

"Um, could we maybe have the first lett—" he began.

"No," said Mr L. "Everyone, it's time for the bonus word. When you've flipped over your test, I'll know you're ready."

Mr L was not going to let Jeffrey out of his sight. Jeffrey knew this. He glanced around the room in a desperate attempt to find some escape. That's when he saw the window.

"Mr L!" his hand shot up. "Mr L, there's a giant hawk outside the window! Look, it's sitting in the tree right there —"

"Jeffrey, finish your test."

"No really, it's there, you gotta see— oh wait, wait, Mr L, wait there's a bunny rabbit under the tree and OH WOW! THE HAWK JUST SWOOPED DOWN AND GRABBED THE BUNNY! It's got it in its talons and it's ripping apart all the fur oh my gosh there's so much blood —"

"Jeffrey," Mr L had positioned himself between Jeffrey and the window, arms crossed over his chest, refusing to turn. "If you do not be quiet and finish your test right now—"

"The bunny has friends!" Jeffrey was almost standing now, craning his neck to see better, "Mr L, they're popping up from their holes now and they're taking on the hawk! Oh Mr L, I know we've got a spelling test and that's super important but you've never seen anything like this! The papa bunny is heaving the little baby bunnies at the hawk like grenades, he's lobbing them and they're attacking mid-air but the hawk is dodging— oh wait, wait, no the hawk

13

dropped it! The hawk dropped the first bunny that got mauled— I think that's the momma bunny— the hawk dove back down to get it and the bunnies have pounced! They're tackling the hawk, oh wow they're beating him to a pulp with their little paws— oh my, Mr L, he's not going down easy, but there are so many of them, feathers and blood and bones and— no way— THERE'S ANOTHER HAWK!"

The class did not hear what happened when the second hawk entered the fight, because at that moment Mr L snapped the shade down on the classroom window. Unfortunately for Mr L, in order to do so he had to turn around and yank the string. That was all the time that Jeffrey needed.

Jeffrey got one out of twenty on his spelling test, which was one higher than he'd gotten last week. He couldn't help but brag as he left school that day, especially to Albert, who had spelled "adventurous" with a second E instead of a U. "Adventurous" was the only word Jeffrey got correct. That's because, he explained, it was the easiest. Spelling was a total piece of cake.

3

ALBERT'S HOMEWORK

Albert was having a tolerably good day at school. In fact, it was about as enjoyable as a day at school could probably be, especially a Tuesday.

Lunch was Sloppy Joes, which were not as good as tacos, but better than anything else served in the cafeteria. At gym they played flag football, which Albert enjoyed way more than soccer. Then, during second break, Albert's friend Jake found a wriggling pile of beetle larva in a mound of mulch, which they happily relocated into a third grader's cubby. But the real reason for Albert's high spirits had happened that morning, right at the end of math class.

Just as Mr L finished a lesson on fractions, he was interrupted by Porge's mom, who came to drop off Porge's forgotten lunch. Mr L stepped outside to chat with her and by the time he reentered, it was already time to start the next class. The significance of this was not lost on Albert. He locked eyes with Leo, Jake, and even Greg, and they were all thinking the same thing: Mr L had forgotten to assign math homework.

Class after class went by, as three o'clock dismissal neared, and Albert grew more and more assured in his victory. All throughout last period, instead of listening to Mr L's discussion about sixteenth century explorers, Albert dreamed of what he would do with all the extra time in his afternoon. With no math homework, the options were limitless.

He could play video games. He could watch t.v.. He could play video games *and* watch t.v.. He could play video games on his iPad, watch a YouTuber play the same video game on his mom's iPhone, and also watch t.v. *at the same time*. Albert shivered. It was all too exciting.

Then Mr L shut the history book. Albert hardly breathed as he shoved books into his backpack, then jumped to his feet and ran for the door. This might just be the best day of his entire life.

It was at that moment— when Albert reached this exultant conclusion— that he heard a terrible sound. Jeffrey cleared his throat.

Albert turned, a look of horror on his face. Jeffrey hadn't packed yet. He sat in his desk with his hand in the air. Albert wanted to tackle him, stuff his fist in his mouth, anything— but it was too late.

"Yes, Jeffrey?" said Mr L.

"Sorry Mr L," said Jeffrey, as silence gripped the classroom, "but I think you forgot to assign our math homework."

Jeffrey followed up his comment with an apologetic giggle; he didn't want to seem too forward, to dare correct the teacher. But Mr L was nothing if not thankful for Jeffrey's intervention.

"Oh, of course," he said. "Sorry boys, I've been so scattered today. Yes, take out your homework notebooks now. No, no one leaves yet. Albert sit back down. Okay, problem set thirty-four."

"Evens or odds?"

The question came from the back of Albert's throat, a desperate rasp.

"All of it," Mr L said. "It's only twenty-five problems, don't worry."

"Thanks Mr L," said Jeffrey, scribbling away in his notebook. "We wouldn't want to miss that problem set!"

"No, we wouldn't," agreed Mr L. Then, after a quick survey of the expressions on his students' faces, he added, "You know, you all should thank Jeffrey for reminding me. Otherwise, you would've had both problem sets tomorrow."

"Haha oh boy, can you imagine?" giggled Jeffrey.

"But, it's not tomorrow," said Albert, his voice hollow. "It's today."

"Yes, and that's your homework for today. Make sure to write it down before you leave, Albert."

Albert still stood in the doorway. Mr L looked at him,

until he, unwillingly, moved step by step back to his desk. Somehow he found himself in his chair. His notebook reemerged from his bag. His pencil, shaking, began to write: "Tuesday Homework: Math P.S. 34." The pencil broke in his grip. Albert heard a soft gurgling sound from the desk beside him, that grated on his ears like nails on a chalkboard. Jeffrey was still giggling.

"Think of that," he was saying to himself. "Two problem sets in one night! Dodged a bullet there, oh man am I glad I remembered!"

"Jeffrey," Albert said slowly, carefully, solemnly, "I will literally punch you."

"Hey that's not nice. Mr L—"

"You can tell the teacher. You can tell your mother. You can tell anyone. But it won't matter. Because wherever you go, I'll find you. And I will punch you."

Jeffrey paused, then stuck out his bottom lip.

"I'd like to see you try, fat boy."

Albert tried.

Mr L had to separate Albert and Jeffrey shortly afterwards, as Jeffrey wiped back tears and called Albert a bully. Albert shed no tears but continued to glare at his adversary.

"Albert," Mr L said, "that was entirely uncalled for, jumping on a fellow student like that. What do you say to Jeffrey?"

"I will not apologize," said Albert, "because Jeffrey has taken away my will to live."

"I'm sorry?"

"He has ruined my afternoon. He has literally ruined my life."

Albert emitted a groan which seemed to be summoned from the depths of his very being.

"You are being dramatic," Mr L said. "Is all this really about homework?"

"Yes," said Albert.

"Well get over it. Time to go home, and no more fighting in my class. Really."

"Hear that?" said Jeffrey, his voice barely above a whisper as Mr L urged them both out the door. "Mr L says to get over it, you big baby."

"I will get over it," Albert said gravely, "only after I host a party at your funeral. With colored streamers and a piñata. A piñata that is an oversized replica of your head, and full of king-sized Reese's."

"Reese's are my favorite," said Jeffrey, offended.

"And you will get none. Because you will be buried beneath me, as I eat all the Reese's myself, and dance over your grave. Only then will I ever smile again."

"Whatever, weirdo."

Jeffrey snickered as he dodged Albert's lunge, then as Albert's backpack flew up over his shoulders— carried by his momentum— and temporarily incapacitated him, Jeffrey sprinted up to the parking lot. Albert regained his balance in time to see Jeffrey disappear safely into his mom's minivan. The window rolled down as the van pulled away, and a little pale hand poked out, then waved.

"How was school?" asked Albert's mother, as she

helped him into the car.

"Terrible."

"Oh come on, it wasn't that bad."

"Literally the worst day of my life."

"That's what you said yesterday."

"It was true yesterday. And now it's true today."

"Well, what was so bad?"

"I have So. Much. Homework."

Albert thrust his head against the seat of the car and reflected on the cruelty of the world. He continued to reflect on the world's cruelty as he lay face down in the front hall of his house, then as he sprawled for exactly three minutes on each stair in his slow ascent to the second floor, groaning the entire time. Finally, he made it to his room, then to his desk, where he stared at the blank surface of wood for another fifteen minutes before allowing his forehead to connect with it over and over again, moaning at each hit.

"Albert! You're going to hurt yourself!" his mother said from the doorway.

"The, pain, is, better, than, math," Albert said between thumps.

"Just do your twenty-five problems, they really won't take long, then you can enjoy yourself! I'm making chicken and rice for dinner."

"I, hate, chicken, and, rice."

"Or mope about it. It's your decision. You know, you'll enjoy life a lot more, Albert, when you just accept that sometimes you have to do things you don't want to do."

Albert did not respond. This was his mom's favorite saying. He heard it at least three times a day. After her footsteps receded down the stairs, he paused his efforts to inflict pain. Albert began to calculate. He knew that all electronics and remotes were stored in the off-limits cabinet of the kitchen, with the lock that would only be removed after he finished his homework. There was no getting around this household rule, and blatant falsehoods did not work, as his homework notebook and math book would both be carefully scrutinized before he even got close to the blissful cupboard. But there might be getting around the lock.

It was a bicycle lock and only his mother knew the combination. Albert had heard something from his father about how bicycle locks were sometimes sawed into, and bicycles stolen. Albert knew of an old jagged hand saw collecting dust in their shed. All he needed was a diversion.

The doorbell rang. It was Jake, asking if Albert would be able to come to the park and play. Albert's mom said of course he could, only he had to finish his homework first. Albert watched this interaction from the stairs. Then, he asked politely whether he might have a moment alone with Jake in his room, to discuss a particularly difficult math problem. His mother agreed, but set a timer for five minutes. Due to prior experience, most things in Albert's life were confined to the timer.

"I need more beetle larva," said Albert, as soon as the door was shut.

"How much?" said Jake. He was not one to ask for reasons why.

"As much as you can get."

"I can scrounge near the park. I think it's the season for them, but I can't promise anything like we found at break."

"Do your best."

"What's in it for me?"

"Two quarters," said Albert, "and another two tomorrow, provided the larva is delivered in the next twenty minutes. Back stoop."

Jake happily accepted the cash and said goodbye to Albert's mother on his way out.

Albert sat and mused. He drew a diagram of the velocity and power that would need to be leveraged by the saw to break through the sturdy wire lock. He was confident in his abilities. He then sketched a fairly detailed depiction of Jeffrey wandering into a pit of venomous snakes. Twenty minutes had passed. Then forty. Albert ran downstairs on the pretext of getting fresh air. His mother set the timer for five minutes.

Sure enough, there was a little pile of wriggling larvae on the stoop. Albert nodded, then spent the rest of his break time in the shed. With the saw secured beneath his shirt, and the larvae in his pocket, he reentered the house.

"How's your homework coming?" asked his mother cheerfully as she stirred the rice.

"Terrible," said Albert, as he stomped upstairs.

Before he entered his room, however, he made two key

stops. Now it was a waiting game. As he waited, he sharpened the saw on the metal part of his bed frame, running it carefully along the edge to make the least amount of noise. He was listening intently for something downstairs. Then came the first scream.

Albert sprang into action. He sprinted down to the kitchen and knelt beside the cabinet, then went furiously to work on the wire of the lock. Nothing. Instead, the saw teeth bent backwards with each thrust. He paused, glanced to the hallway, desperate. A second scream came from the bathroom; he didn't have much time. He punched the side of the cupboard in frustration.

Albert paused. He suddenly had a new idea.

Two hours later, Albert and his parents sat down to dinner. His mother was still rattled by the discovery of two colorless beetle larvae crawling on her iPhone and then, after she'd disposed of them outside and went to wash her hands, another fat larva on the handle of the sink in the bathroom. She suspected foul play but could not hope to pin it on Albert; he'd been in his room the entire afternoon, quietly and diligently doing his work.

"Are you almost finished, honey? You've worked so hard."

"Got about an hour left," grunted Albert, shoveling chicken and rice into his open mouth.

"That's my boy," said Albert's dad.

Albert grunted again. He finished his food and ran back up to his room while his parents did the dishes.

When they were almost done, Albert's father remarked that, while he didn't quite agree with the placement, it was certainly interesting to have moved the floor plant from the front hall to right beside the kitchen cabinet. Albert's mother hadn't noticed; she'd been distracted by the thought of the larvae. Now, upon examination, she agreed it looked odd and couldn't imagine why she'd done it. She picked up the plant to move it back. That's when Albert's parents discovered the jagged hole in the cabinet, above a little pile of sawdust.

Albert was soundly punished. But the day was not wasted; in the time he had to himself in his room with his iPad, he had succeeded in logging on and punching Jeffrey's avatar twenty-six times. He went to sleep grounded, but with a smile.

4

GREG GOES DRIVING

"Pretty fast," Greg was saying at lunch. "I don't know exactly, maybe like fifty or seventy miles per hour."

"Were you on the highway?" asked Porge.

"Not the highway, like a smaller road but still not that small. I've done it like a million times, it's easy."

"Stick shift or automatic?" inquired Jake, who knew something about cars.

"A bit of both," Greg shrugged. "Sometimes I mix them up, keeps it interesting. Depends on how you want the ride to feel."

"What is your ride again?" said Leo, exchanging glances with Jake.

"My mom's Honda Odyssey. I mean it's no Ferrari, but it can boogie."

"And she lets you drive the car," Leo said slowly,

"alone?"

"Yeah, you know," Greg shifted a bit in his seat, chewed on a bite of sandwich. "She lets me take it out for a spin now and again. Got to practice for when I get my license."

"Wow," said Jake, "that's actually super cool."

"Yeah?" said Greg, "Yeah, I guess it is."

"I wanna learn to drive," Porge mumbled.

"One day I'll teach you," said Greg generously.

"Really?" said Leo, "You'd teach us? You would?"

"Yeah sure, why not?"

"This weekend."

"I'm kind of busy this weekend."

"Wait, but are your parents going to the school picnic?" Leo asked, suddenly excited. "Mine are, and this year it's only adults. It's from three until five on Saturday, so we'll come around then."

"That's a good idea," said Greg, trying to think quickly. "But they'll probably take the mini van and—"

"So let's drive your dad's car," said Jake.

"Okay but I only know how to drive the mini—"

"Dude, this is so cool," said Leo. "I'm going to tell everyone."

"I can't wait!" said Porge.

"Three o'clock on Saturday," Jake confirmed. "We'll be at Greg's. I mean, you *can* drive, right?"

There was a moment's pause. Greg was given this merciful opportunity to back out, though of course it was on Jake's terms, and would've been a humiliating blow.

Especially since he had been bragging about driving for two straight days. But now Greg began to think, how hard could driving actually be? Last weekend his mom had let him sit on her lap and hold the wheel, after he begged for hours, because he'd been playing SuperRacer7 on Xbox with the new plastic pedal controllers and wanted to see if he could do it on a real car. That was the seed of truth from which his story had extravagantly grown. And now he figured, why not? Driving should be easy. He could teach the other boys, he would show Jake who probably didn't believe him, and everyone would be talking about how cool he really was.

"Oh yeah," he said. "I can totally drive."

And so Greg's fate was sealed.

Jake, Porge, and Leo wasted no time in spreading the word. Crowds of well-wishers gathered around Greg, assuring him they'd be present on the big day. He enjoyed his newfound popularity and began to believe that he deserved it. He explained driving mechanics to wide-eyed groups of third graders, opined about his favorite car models, demonstrated specific techniques while miming the steering wheel and adding exhaust noises by spitting— all knowledge gathered from long days in the basement with SuperRacer7— and he answered any question with the utmost confidence.

There were doubters among the boys, but Leo and Jake insisted that they come Saturday to see for real. Most of their parents would be at the picnic, and many of them lived in the same neighborhood, so they would have more than enough time to walk over and learn all of Greg's driving secrets, to watch him drive all on his own, all by himself, before the picnic ended.

Saturday morning came. Greg felt suddenly queasy. He had been escorted to the parking lot with a chorus of cheers after school on Friday; he had waved at his adoring fans as he climbed into the same grey Odyssey he would again be climbing into today. Only this time, he would be at the wheel. He panicked.

Unfortunately, despite Greg's tear-filled protests, his parents still went to the picnic. They left Greg in charge of his younger siblings, something they had just begun to do, hoping that the meager amount of responsibility would help him mature. This afternoon was especially risk free, as they'd only be gone for about two hours, and it was the middle of the day. Greg clutched their feet and begged them to stay. They refused and said he would be fine. Then, to add insult to injury, they took his dad's car and left the Odyssey in the driveway.

The doorbell rang at 3:15. Leo was standing there with a big grin. Already a group of boys had gathered around the car, and more filtered in from the road.

"You ready?" Leo said.

"Duh," said Greg. "I was born ready."

He grabbed the keys and went out. His two younger siblings had been lured into the basement to watch Lion King, then he'd— like any good babysitter— locked them down there. The basement didn't have any front-facing windows, so he was confident his drive would remain undetected.

"You sure your parents are okay with this?" said Leo, as Greg strutted to the car.

"Oh yeah," Greg assured him. "They let me do it all the time."

"Thanks for this, Greg!" said Porge. "I've always wanted to learn how to drive."

"It's easy," Greg said. "A baby could do it."

He tried the door. It wouldn't open.

"I think you gotta unlock it first," Jake said.

"Yeah duh," Greg shot back, then addressed the crowd of twenty boys, gathered on his front lawn:

"Lesson number one. You take the key," he held it high for all to see, "then you press this button and unlock the door."

The lights flicked and the car beeped. There was a smattering of applause. Greg gave a brief bow then entered the car.

"Roll down the window," Leo said, tapping on the glass, "so we can still hear you when you're inside."

Greg nodded, then pressed the window button. Nothing happened. He pressed several times, harder, but still nothing.

"You gotta start the engine," Jake was mouthing.

Greg nodded as if to say he knew that, then looked for the place to insert the key. It wasn't in the cup holders, or the middle of the steering wheel, or under his seat—

"There!" Leo was saying, and Jake and Porge were pointing too. Then Greg saw the ignition, smiled, and slid in the key. He gave it a twist and the engine turned then purred, as only a nine-year-old Honda Odyssey can purr. The crowd cheered.

"Is he actually going to do it?" Porge whispered to Leo.

"Of course he is," said Leo; "it's Greg."

The window rolled down and Greg thrust his head out.

"You guys gotta give me some space," he snapped. "I don't wanna kill anyone."

The boys stepped back. Except for Jake, who figured Greg might need more help getting started. He was right.

"Put your foot on the brake," he instructed Greg.

The engine revved loudly. The crowd "oohed" and "ahhed."

"No, the other pedal," Jake said, "and hold it down."

"I know what I'm doing," snapped Greg.

"Okay then you know that once your foot's on the brake, you gotta move that stick thing there to the letter D."

"Duh," said Greg, and he shifted the car to drive.

It was at this point that Jake too backed away.

Greg's house was on a slope, and his driveway went downhill to the road. Luckily for him, the car had been parked with its back to the house, front facing down the driveway. To their right the road went on until it ended in a cul-de-sac, a wide circle surrounded by houses. To the left the road turned back into the neighborhood. Greg decided he would go right, circle the cul-de-sac, then bring the car back to where he found it. Simple.

He lifted his foot from the brake, slightly, and the car

started forward. He jammed his foot down and it jerked to a stop. The onlookers began to chant "Greg", "Greg", "Greg," and he gained some confidence. He held the steering wheel with both hands, both near the top, both gripping so tight his knuckles were white. It was all he could do to reach down for the pedals and also see over the dash, but by sitting as far up on the seat as possible and craning his neck, he could manage.

He lifted his foot and pressed down again. Then again. In this stuttering, jerking motion, he slowly and steadily made it down the driveway.

"He's at the road!" Porge yelled, to a chorus of cheers. Greg waved. He yanked the steering wheel to the right and inched onto the street.

"He's turning!" yelled Porge.

Now Greg had confidence; he had reached the street. Time to move his foot from the brake. Time to press the accelerator. Unfortunately, this was another part about cars of which he had no experience except for those long hours playing SuperRacer7. On those plastic pedals, there was only one thing to do with the accelerator.

Greg shoved his foot down, hard. The Odyssey roared and the boys around the car scattered. It shot straight at the cul-de-sac, increasing in speed.

Greg breathed quickly. He knew that the one thing he should not do— given his SuperRacer7 expertise— was take his foot off the accelerator. So as the dead end neared, he kept pressing down and yanked the wheel to one side.

The boys watched the van speed into the court then twirl wildly around twice, nearly tipping over. They "oohed" in unison. The van swung with such force that Greg lost his footing on the accelerator, and then in trying to regain it accidentally stomped on the brake. There was a piercing screech. The crowd "ahhed". The car shuddered then rolled slowly forward, dribbling back toward Greg's house.

The boys jumped up and down. Greg had done it. Even Jake and Leo smiled; they'd anticipated disaster, but somehow success for Greg wasn't half-bad to see. He was waving as the van approached, then passed the driveway. It jerked to an abrupt halt as he stomped the brake again.

"Alright," said Jake happily, coming alongside. "You gotta hold the brake and move that stick thing to R. It stands for "Reverse." Then you can put it back in the driveway the same way."

Greg complied, then made a show of glancing over his shoulder as he turned the car, carefully, into the driveway. Boys on either side shouted out directions for left and right, and Jake helped guide him in applying the brake and — very softly— tapping the accelerator, until after fifteen minutes of starting and stopping the car was back in its original spot. The audience went crazy with approval.

It might've been Greg's proudest moment. He rolled up the window, careful to leave everything as he had found it, then changed the stick to N, which he assumed meant "Nothing," or "No Power," as opposed to P, which probably meant "Power." Then he leapt out the car and took a gallant bow.

When he arose, he saw the faces of his admirers had turned from jubilant to shocked, then horrified. He turned around. The empty minivan was rolling down the driveway, picking up speed. It shot across the street and smashed into the neighbor's parked Mercedes. The onlookers scattered. Greg stood by himself, blinking, in his front yard.

It was many years until Greg was left alone unsupervised again.

5

LATE TO CLASS

"And that is why the square root of sixteen can be further divided— Oh, hello Jeffrey. You're late."

"Yes, Mr L, excuse me, very sorry sir."

Jeffrey shrugged off his backpack and hung up his coat in his cubby. Mr L stood by the board and seemed to be waiting.

"Do you have a late-slip?"

"Oh! No sir, I'm sorry sir, I completely forgot, see we were held up by traffic on the road and I rushed down. There was this motorcycle accident and—"

"On the highway?"

"No sir, one of the streets in my neighborhood, this little girl got her foot run over and we—"

"That's terrible!"

"Yes and my mom wanted to stop but I told her I had

to get to school on time, so we only slowed down, but I think someone else had called the police so hopefully—"

"Alright, alright, sit down Jeffrey. Open your math book to page seventy-six."

Jeffrey sat down and got to work. Mr L looked at him for one moment more, then continued with the lesson.

The next day, ten minutes after class had begun, Mr L was interrupted again. Jeffrey walked straight toward him this time, with a little pink slip of paper in his hand.

"Overslept?" read Mr L. "That was your reason for being late?"

"Oh it wasn't me sir," Jeffrey said earnestly. "It was my mom. See she's on this new pain medication because she twisted her ankle when playing tennis last Tuesday and normally she takes her sleep pills after dinner but last night she forgot, so she took her pills after dessert, but then realized she actually had taken them after dinner too! So she was angry for like five minutes then fell asleep. And she was still out cold this morning, I had to pour two big bowls of cold water over her face to wake her up, and even then I didn't get to school on time so—"

"Jeffrey. Take a seat."

The next day Jeffrey was late again.

"Sir," he said, interrupting math for the third time that week, "you'll never guess what happened—"

"You can tell me during break," said Mr L.

The class exchanged glances. Jeffrey had been late one too many times and lost his recess. Jeffrey hung up his coat and found his seat.

"So what happened this morning?" Mr L said three periods later, as Jeffrey watched the others go out to play.

"Well, we left the house on time," Jeffrey explained. "I made sure of it, sir. But then there was this giant tree on the road, right in front of our driveway, so we had to get out this chainsaw and—"

"Jeffrey, I called your mom."

"Oh?"

"She says she dropped you off on time, every day this week. Not only that, but she's dropped you off *early*. Because you insisted on being here fifteen minutes before the normal drop-off time. Care to explain?"

Jeffrey suddenly became very interested in sharpening his pencil.

"Jeffrey?"

"Um, no."

"No what?"

"If it's all the same to you, sir, I wouldn't care to explain."

"Well it's not all the same to me, because you are my student, and you've been missing class, and telling lies."

"I'll be here on time tomorrow. I promise."

Mr L looked hard at Jeffrey, who held his gaze with a touch of stubborn resolve. Experience had taught Mr L that direct investigation during situations that involved lying was not likely to get him the truth. More often than not, it got him more lies. It was better to wait. All would be revealed. So he nodded, and Jeffrey seemed to relax.

Mr L released Jeffrey for break, but Jeffrey said he'd

rather sit out the whole punishment, because he felt so bad. This warmed up Mr L to him considerably. Not only that, but Jeffrey stayed in after lunch to help Mr L sharpen pencils. He even waited after school to help tidy up the classroom, staying a full fifteen minutes past dismissal.

"See you tomorrow, Jeffrey," said Mr L with a smile, as Jeffrey waved and went out the door.

The next day Jeffrey was late. Mr L proceeded with the math lesson, but after five minutes he put his marker down. This situation had gone far enough. He instructed the class to do silent work, because he had to make a phone call. He stepped outside with the intention of once again calling Jeffrey's mom.

Rounding the corner, he almost knocked over Jeffrey. The boy had been standing just out of sight, facing the wall, staring at his watch.

"Oh! Mr L!" he said, "Sorry, I was just rushing down to class, you'll never believe what happened to me this morning—"

"Jeffrey—"

"I really really wanted to be on time, after I promised you and—"

"Jeffrey—"

"But then this enormous bear with rabies—"

"Jeffrey!"

"Totally foaming at the mouth, stepped right in front of me on my way to the classroom and roared. I think it was protecting its young, so I had to dodge and hide and —"

"Jeffrey, what on earth are you doing out here?"

"I, well, I was— uh, listening, sir."

"Listening?"

"I didn't want to miss the lesson."

Mr L stared at him.

"Jeffrey, get inside. We'll talk about this at break."

During break, Jeffrey was as apologetic as before. He promised to stay in for all that break and the next one, and also to stay after school to help clean up again. In fact, if Mr L insisted, he would do that for the entire rest of the week. At this point, Mr L was more than suspicious.

"Jeffrey," he said, "why don't you want to go to break? And why have you been avoiding morning line-up?"

"Excuse me, sir? There is nothing I would like more than to go out and play with my friends."

"Okay, you can go."

"I'm sorry?"

"I forgive you. Go on, go out to break. You're released."

"But sir, that's hardly fair. After all, I was very late today."

"Don't worry about it."

"And after my promise yesterday—"

"Go on, leave."

"And I told terrible lies—"

"Water under the bridge."

"Really I can't—"

"Sure you can. Get out of here. Go play."

Mr L crossed the room and opened the door. Jeffrey

remained in his desk. It did not escape Mr L's notice that fifteen feet away, just within sight of the classroom, Albert leaned against a tree.

"Mr L, I'd rather not," said Jeffrey in a small voice.

"Well then," Mr L shut the door, "care to tell me what's going on?"

"No."

"Something to do with Albert."

Jeffrey jerked around in his chair, locking eyes with Mr L.

"I never said anything!" he cried, "I didn't tell you anything!"

"It's okay, you can tell me what's going on."

"You can't protect me! No one can protect me!"

"Jeffrey, there's nothing Albert can do."

"My mouth is shut!"

"Do I need to go outside and bring Albert in here?"

Jeffrey let out a shriek and Mr L knew he had him. He stood right over Jeffrey's desk.

"Tell me what's going on."

Jeffrey made an effort to open his mouth. Quietly, so that Mr L had to lean in to hear, he whispered:

"Mr L, I don't want to go to prison."

"You're not going to prison."

"I owe Albert a large sum of money."

"Money? Why?"

"I made a series of poorly thought out bets. If I don't pay up he's gonna get his family to break every bone in my body."

"Okay, that's ridiculous."

"But Mr L, snitches get stitches."

"Jeffrey where did you hear that? Never mind, don't answer. Look, you can tell Albert that snitches do not get stitches in my classroom."

"And even if I somehow survive the beating, I'll be bankrupt!"

"Okay Jeffrey, how much do you owe Albert?"

"Sixteen dollars."

Mr L put his face into his hand.

"Really?" he said.

"Yes!" Jeffrey shrieked, "It all started last week, when we bet fifty cents that I could climb a tree higher than him. I didn't know he was such a good climber, how could I know? Then I tried again and again to get it back and he kept offering double or nothing and now he's gonna get his Italian cousins to take me out if I don't pay up!"

"Jeffrey, relax. I'm not getting involved in this. Just do not be late to class again, okay? You can't avoid Albert forever. He's not going to hurt you. And neither are his Italian cousins. Just explain that you don't have the money, and next time don't make bets that you can't pay. Got it? Now go to break."

Jeffrey stood, slowly. He moved toward the door of the classroom like a condemned man to a gallows. At the threshold he turned back to Mr L, in one final plea for mercy. Mr L frowned. Jeffrey averted his eyes, then walked through the door.

Mr L watched through the window as Jeffrey and

Albert talked by the tree. Jeffrey seemed to be waving his hands around. Then, miraculously, Albert smiled. They shook hands. Looking around, they called Jake over.

Jake stood at the base of the tree with his arms crossed, as Jeffrey and Albert both scrambled for the lower branches. Mr L was confused, then, as Albert swung himself up and continued to climb, realized his error. He was out the door a second later, as Albert was already halfway up the tree, and he yelled:

"Albert, Jeffrey, come here, now!"

Albert let himself down and shuffled toward Mr L. Jake moved away. Then Mr L looked around. Jeffrey had disappeared. He wasn't anywhere near the tree, nor the classrooms, nor the field. He was gone.

"Where'd Jeffrey go?" he asked Albert.

"I don't know," Albert moaned, "but he owes me thirty-two dollars."

6

THE FAT AND THE SPAZ

"Hey Porge," said Jake, "trade me one of your cookies for this granola bar."

"No way," said Porge. "Over my dead body."

"You have six cookies!"

"Yeah, because I save them up from other lunches and eat them all at once."

"Alright, fatty."

"I'm not fat!"

The other boys at the table sniggered. It was universally known that Porge was indeed fat. That's how he got his nickname, Porge. His full name, Gordon, had turned into "Gordey-Porgey," then just simply, "Porge." He was actually the skinniest boy in the fifth grade. But his attitude toward food, and indeed his general attitude toward life itself, had given him the reputation of fatness.

Porge didn't really mind. He protested out of habit. Sometimes he became more annoyed, like when he got picked later for teams because of this alleged fatness. He was actually one of the quickest students in the grade. Or, he could've been, if he wasn't so lazy.

"I'm not fat," he was insisting, "I just like cookies."

"I think," Timmy said, "if you were less fat, you would share."

Jake and Leo agreed. Porge shook his head.

"Not wanting to give up good cookies has nothing to do with fatness," he explained. "If you had cookies there's no way you'd trade them for a gross granola bar."

"Maybe if I had one cookie," said Jake. "But six whole cookies? Do you need to eat six whole cookies during one lunch?"

"Yes. Yes I do."

"What's up, losers?" Greg swung onto the bench beside Porge, uninvited, and slammed his lunchbox on the table. "Got lunchables today," he announced as he opened his bag, "sweet."

"Porge doesn't care that you have lunchables," said Jake, "because he's got six cookies."

Greg looked at the neat little stack which Porge had made, so high it was taller than his lunch box.

"Woah," he said. "Look at Fatty McFatso over here with his chubby little cookies."

Porge's face went red. He didn't mind being called fat by those he considered to be friends, but Greg was not in that number. And Greg had a special, intuitive knack for taking things too far.

"I'm not fat," Porge muttered, cramming a cookie into his mouth. "Don't call me fat."

"Sorry, I couldn't hear you because your mouth was full of cookie," Greg said loudly. "All the crumbs were spilling down your seven chins."

"I don't have seven chins," Porge snapped; "I have one normal chin and don't call me fat!"

"Jake called you fat, why don't you get mad at him?"

"Because Jake is my friend!"

"Whatever, fatty."

Porge stood up, glared at Greg, then gave him a push. Greg flailed his arms and pushed back, making Porge trip. There was a general gasp from the surrounding tables. Porge picked himself up, shaking.

"You," he said softly, "you are a spaz."

"No, I'm not," said Greg immediately. "You pushed me first."

"I nudged you," Porge said, "and then you totally spazzed."

"I am not a spaz!" yelled Greg. "You tripped on your own fat!"

"He's gonna spaz again!" Porge announced to the lunchroom, "Spaz! Spaz!"

Greg jumped on Porge's back, trying to get him in a headlock. Porge ran around in a circle, toppling lunchroom chairs, still yelling, "Spaz!" That's when the teachers stepped in. Both boys lost their break.

But word had spread. The whole fifth grade was talking

about how Greg had totally spazzed on Porge at lunch. Everywhere Greg went, boys looked at him and he knew what they were thinking. So he yelled at them to stop thinking he was a spaz. Then they covered their mouths and giggled, saying that he had spazzed again. Greg was getting desperate.

During class, he raised his hand. Mr L was teaching natural history. They were supposed to go on a nature walk to examine trees, but a wasps' nest had been found in a rotting log in the woods, so the walk was deemed too risky. Instead, Mr L skipped the tree unit and gave a lecture on rocks. Greg's question was not about rocks.

"Mr L," he said, "what does 'spaz' mean?"

The question was followed by a smattering of giggles. Greg jerked round in his chair, glaring at his classmates, as if daring them to find this funny. Unfortunately, they now found it even more funny.

"Greg," said Mr L, "that's off-topic."

"But I need to know what it means."

"Hey, I looked up 'spaz' in the dictionary," squealed Porge from the other side of the room. "It says the definition is 'Greg'!"

This comment was received with uproarious laughter, from everyone except Greg and Mr L. Greg jumped out of his desk and tried to get to Porge, yelling at the top of his lungs that he was not a spaz. Mr L slammed his book down on the desk, causing immediate silence.

"That's enough," he barked. "Greg, sit down. A spaz is someone who overreacts. Someone who makes a big deal out of a very small thing. Okay? Got it? Good. Back to rocks."

During second break, Porge led a group of boys in the spaz game, in which you find a spaz and sneak up behind him then say "Spaz!" in a high pitched voice until he spazzes out on you. This game was an instant success with everyone except for Greg, who's participation in it was involuntary.

After school, Greg didn't want his special Tuesday snack. His mother wondered what was wrong, and he burst into tears.

"The boys at school call me names," he said through sobs.

"No, why would they do that?" asked his mother.

"I don't know! It started at lunch when I was nicely talking to Porge and out of nowhere he called me a spaz! So then I defended myself and they said I was even more of a spaz!"

"Well that doesn't sound like Gordon at all, he's such a nice boy. I'll call his mother and speak to her about name calling—"

"No!" Greg said quickly, knowing that direct parental involvement in such disputes would be the nail in the coffin of his reputation. "No! It's okay, mom, I can handle it."

"You are so brave, honey."

"I am. I know."

"Maybe you can try this. When your friends call you names, just smile back at them. Laugh it off and don't react, then they'll get tired and move on. That's just how boys are."

"Okay," Greg smiled through his tears, "I think I will have that snack after all. Thanks mom."

Mothers always know what to say.

"Sup spaz," said Porge, during morning lineup.

Greg erupted in laughter.

"Oh Porge," he said, patting his shoulder, "you are just so funny."

"Don't touch me, spazzo."

"Hah! Spazzo! That's a good one! See I understand now, you're just joking! We are joking!"

Greg laughed even louder. This attracted the attention of the other boys.

"What's Greg spazzing out about now?" said Jake.

"Oh Jake! Classic Jake!" Greg laughed, "That was clever! You're so clever."

"I'm not trying to be clever, what's so funny?"

"Porge is! Porge and his witty little jokes!"

Greg was doubled over now, still laughing. No one else was laughing. It was early in the morning, class started in a couple minutes, and no one was in the mood to laugh.

"Look at what a weirdo Greg is," Porge said. "He's like even more of a spaz than yesterday when he was yelling at us."

"No," said Greg, suddenly serious. "I'm way less of a spaz, because now I'm laughing."

"Yeah, but it's still super weird," said Porge.

"Maybe it's weird but it means I'm not a spaz," Greg snapped back, "because I didn't overreact."

"No," said Porge. "It means you are weird and a spaz. You are a weird spaz."

"Oh yeah?"

"Yeah."

"YEAH?"

Porge took a step back.

"Uh oh," he said to the others. "Here comes the spaz."

Greg shed his backpack to tackle Porge, screaming about how Porge was the fattest person he'd ever met. Porge fought back, and both lost their lunch and both breaks when Mr L arrived at the classroom.

"Come on guys," he said, looking down at the two boys entangled and grunting on the ground. "School hasn't even started yet."

He anticipated a long day, and he was correct. But it was nothing like the next day.

As Greg sat in detention and glared at Porge, he came to a number of conclusions. The first was that a mother's advice could not be trusted in a situation as dire as this. He had tried to laugh it off. The strategy was nice, simple, neat, but it had failed. He needed something more drastic, something that made an impact. And so Greg began to think about other solutions to dire situations. As with most problems in life, he looked to his guiding light to find the true answer: movies.

When his mom asked how the name-calling at school had gone, Greg just grunted. He retired to his room for the remainder of the evening. She figured he would find a way to work it out.

The next day, Porge and the others tried to play the spaz game but they couldn't find Greg anywhere. Porge said he must be hiding, and everyone thought this was very funny. They teased Greg for hiding later in class. Porge announced that he would follow Greg during second break and see exactly where the spaz had built his lair. But Greg wasn't hiding. He was preparing.

During second break he made a show of walking towards the woods. Porge put his finger to his lips then followed at a distance, telling his friends to stay on the field while he entered under the trees.

"Don't want to scare him and make him spaz," he giggled, then crept on alone.

Just beyond the tree line, something jumped out and grabbed his wrist. Greg had been waiting behind a wide trunk.

"Oh no!" Porge squealed excitedly. "Are you going to spaz?"

"No, Porge, I'm not going to spaz," said Greg in a cold voice.

Porge's giggle died in his throat. He looked around but his friends hadn't followed him, they were alone. Greg pulled him by the wrist deeper into the woods.

"What are you doing?" Porge resisted. "Hey stop, let go!"

"Easy there, Porge, don't be a spaz," said Greg softly. "We wouldn't want that now, would we?"

Porge was just about to twist away when he heard a sinister click. Greg was no longer holding his wrist. Instead, there was a metal toy handcuff, the other side of which was attached to the thick branch of a fallen log.

"Hey," he said, "hey what're you doing? Where are you going?"

"I'd be quiet if I were you," said Greg in a hushed voice. "Look where you are before you say anything else."

Porge obeyed. As he did, he grew very stiff. His eyes went wide. He started to tremble, then to shake.

"I wouldn't shake," said Greg from his spot about fifteen feet away. "The less movement, the better."

Porge tried to control himself but he couldn't; next to him, nestled in the log that he was now handcuffed to, was a nest crawling with wasps.

"Greg," he said softly, his voice a trembling whimper, "Greg, please let me go."

"I could let you go," said Greg, "but I want to test you first. You say that I'm a spaz. Well, it looks like you want to shake and scream right now too, but you can't. Don't be a spaz, Porge, don't be a spaz."

Greg took a scissors out of his pocket. He held them up to a string that Porge hadn't noticed, which was attached to a branch above the log. Porge gasped. Hanging from the branch, on the string, was a fist-sized rock. It dangled directly over the wasps' nest.

"Greg, Greg," he said through shuddering breaths. "Don't do this. I'm sorry."

"Say I'm not a spaz," said Greg.

"Greg, you're not a spaz. Please, Greg, please."

The wasps appeared to have noticed his movement. Some hovered in the air, wondering whether this boy was an intruder.

"Greg! I'm allergic!" Porge burst out, unable to control it any longer. "I'm going to *die*!"

Greg, who had been calmly smiling and drinking in every moment of his triumph, dropped the scissors.

"Wait, what?" he said.

"I'm gonna die!" Porge screamed quicker now, shaking all over. "If I get stung, I swell up and can't breathe and die!"

"Well why didn't you tell me?"

"I'm dead!"

Now that there was screaming the wasps really noticed. A third of them took to the air, buzzing loudly. Porge began hyperventilating.

"Behind your wrist there's a button," Greg yelled. "Press it and run, run!"

"They're gonna come after me!" Porge squealed, tears pouring down his face.

"I'll stop them!" Greg cried. "Just go!"

Many things happened at once. Porge pressed the release button and tore his wrist away, sprinting as fast as he could in the direction of the field. Greg, without thinking, did the bravest act he had ever done. He dive-tackled the wasps' nest.

Porge stumbled out of the trees, chest heaving. Not a single wasp had followed him. His friends crowded around with big grins on their faces.

"Oh man what did you do?" one asked. "Can you hear him scream in there? He's going crazy."

"He's totally spazzing out!" said another. "Let's go see!"

"No," Porge said, "no."

There was something in his voice that made the others pause. The sounds continued.

"What do you mean? Listen to him freak out!"

"I didn't know a human could make sounds like that, it's like a dying piglet."

"We gotta see! Let's play spaz!"

"I will never play spaz again," said Porge, "and Greg is not a spaz," he paused, wiped away a tear. "Greg is a hero."

He ran to tell Mr L what was happening in the woods. Mr L grabbed two other teachers and they rushed out to the rescue. As predicted, it was indeed a long day.

Greg recovered after about a week. A very painful week. But he did not regret what he had done, not at all. Nor did Porge ever tell anyone how they had come to that wasps' nest in the woods. So in the end, Greg's plan worked.

He was never called a spaz by Porge again.

7

CHARLIE GETS IN TROUBLE

Charlie stood next to Mr L's desk, patiently waiting as Mr L arranged his papers and marked where the class had left off. Mr L noticed him and looked up.

"Yes, Charlie?"

"Hi sir, I was wondering, since I have an important baseball practice on Thursday, could I have the homework now, ahead of time? That way I can make sure I get it done."

"Charlie, today is Monday, I don't know what the homework for Thursday will be."

"It's okay, sir," said Charlie politely; "I can wait."

Mr L watched him as he stood quietly beside the desk.

"Charlie," he said, "why don't you go outside to play? It's break."

"Yes sir, but I need the homework for—"

"Charlie."

"Yes sir?"

"Go outside. I'll give you the homework later."

"Okay sir."

The tone of Mr L's voice made it clear that he was not inclined to negotiate. Charlie grabbed a book from his desk and positioned himself right outside the classroom door. This way, if Mr L suddenly thought of what Thursday's homework was, he would know where to find him. Other boys ran past in groups of twos and threes, and there was a kickball game going on at the field.

"Charlie! Psst, Charlie! Come here."

Charlie looked up to see Jake, poking his head around the corner of the building. Experience of Jake taught him that when Jake was poking his head around the corner of anything, Charlie should not be involved.

"Oh no, that's alright," he said. "I'm reading."

"Get over here. Now."

Charlie looked around him. There was no one else. He even glanced back into the classroom; Mr L was on the phone.

"I really shouldn't—" he began, when Jake darted forward and yanked him back around the building with him.

"You're filthy!" cried Charlie.

"Shush. Listen up. I have a job for you."

"No, thank you."

Charlie tried to leave but Jake held his shoulder. From the waist down Jake was covered in wet mud, so thick

Charlie couldn't even see his pants or shoes.

"Charlie, it's not just me," Jake's tone of voice changed. "It's almost our whole class. We're desperate. You're the only one who can help."

Charlie was not a bad boy. He had a chronic fear of getting in trouble, but he did have more than the usual store of love for his common man. Something in Jake's eyes convinced him that his classmate, however naughty, was indeed telling the truth.

"Okay," he said, with hesitation, "tell me what you need, and I'll see if I can do it."

"Great. Follow me."

Jake led the way along the outskirts of the field to a portion of the recess lot called "the woods." A sloped hill surrounded the field and here, in the back corner of the lot, it was covered with a fairly dense thicket of trees. The boys were forbidden to play within these trees, where teachers watching recess could not see them, but this rule was hardly ever enforced and so went completely ignored. Still, Charlie hesitated.

"We aren't supposed to go in the woods," he said.

"No one's looking, it's fine," said Jake, pushing him forward.

Charlie, to his own surprise, allowed himself to be pushed. Maybe it was Jake's attitude, or his abnormal dirtiness, but whatever it was, Charlie could not help but feel curious.

Jake led him toward a small opening between two trunks, where two fifth graders stepped out to block them, nodding suspiciously at Charlie. Jake announced that Charlie was with him and, though still frowning, the fifth graders moved aside. Jake moved on through the trunks and Charlie followed into a wall of thick pine branches. These he pushed out of the way, then froze.

Beneath his feet was an enormous pit. It stretched at least twenty feet deep, though it was difficult to tell exactly, due to networks of exposed roots and crowds of industrious fifth graders who worked at the walls with pickaxes and shovels. The bottom was obscured by a seething floor of mushy mud. Standing in the mud, so far down that Charlie could just make out their heads and shoulders, a pack of fifth graders from Charlie's class yelled and furiously tried to bail out standing water.

"So here's the situation," Jake explained, "for the last couple weeks we've been trying to dig a hole to China. It was difficult breaking ground with all the tree roots but we've made good progress, as you can see. Unfortunately, earlier today we hit a thick metal object that Greg insisted must be buried treasure. Leo said that if it was, it definitely belonged to some long lost Chinese emperor. Probably worth millions. So we attacked it with the shovels but—"

"Where did you get the shovels?" said Charlie, his voice small.

"From home. Amazing what fits in a backpack when no one's checking. So we attacked it with the shovels but turns out it wasn't treasure, it was a water pipe. Started just spraying everywhere. Now Timmy's jammed his thumb in the crack to stop the flow, and everyone's doing their best to bail out, but who knows what'll happen when we have to get back to class?"

Charlie could just see Timmy crouched over something metal at the bottom of the pit.

"His thumb?"

"See that's where you come in, we need—"

"Oh, it's Charlie!" cried a voice from somewhere below. A cheer rang out from the pit as the fifth graders paused their labors to wave.

"Thanks, Charlie!"

"We knew we could count on you!"

"Yeah Charlie!"

"I'm not involved in this—" Charlie tried to say, but Jake interrupted.

"We need you to get Mr L's roll of duct tape."

"Duct tape?"

"We have to patch the pipe and block the water."

"With duct tape?"

"I'm sorry, do you have a better idea?"

Charlie did not. Nor did he want anything to do with this excavation.

"I can't," he said, "I can't help you. Sorry. No can do. I gotta go back and read my book and get my homework for Thursday."

"Charlie, Charlie, Charlie." Jake shook his head. "You don't understand do you? This whole thing's gonna blow up."

"Blow up?"

"Not literally." That was a different voice. Charlie

turned to see Leo climbing out of the hole, similarly covered in mud from the waist down. "You've told him the situation, Jake?"

"He knows what he has to do," said Jake.

"Sorry, but I'm not doing anything," Charlie insisted. "You guys are crazy and you're all going to get in so much trouble—"

"More trouble than you could even imagine," Leo said softly. Charlie's eyes were wide. There was a quiet threat in those words.

"Well, you shouldn't have dug the hole, it's against the rules," he stammered.

"This goes beyond the rules," said Leo. "You think that pipe's connected to nothing? No way. Timmy takes his thumb out of that crack and in fifteen minutes half the neighborhood behind the school is out of water."

"Is that how it works?"

"And then come the floods. We're talking thousands of dollars in damages," said Leo, "maybe even millions."

"This has nothing to do with me," said Charlie quickly, turning to run. Jake held him fast.

"No, let him go, Jake," said Leo casually, "because Charlie, when word gets out about what happened here, they're going to want names. And they'll get them. They'll get the names of every single boy involved. Every one."

Charlie looked around him in horror. Some of the fifth graders who had paused work to wave were still looking up. Some still called out "Yay Charlie!" and expressed how grateful they were for his help. He glanced back at Leo. He could barely speak, he was breathing so hard:

"So, much, trouble."

"Not if word never gets out," Leo corrected him.

"But, how?"

"Duct tape," said Jake.

Three minutes later, Charlie was shivering outside the classroom door. Mr L was still inside on his phone. Leo and Jake had assured Charlie that he was the perfect operative for the job; he wasn't muddy and was the least suspicious person in their whole class. All he had to do was ask Mr L an innocent question, then when he wasn't looking, steal the duct tape right off of his desk.

"I refuse to steal," Charlie had said, retaining any scrap of honor he could.

"But you won't be stealing," Jake argued, "just borrowing."

"Borrowing without permission *is* stealing," Charlie said.

"Not if you give it back," Jake replied.

Charlie did not agree with this logic. But desperate times called for desperate measures. If Jake was correct, he could take the duct tape then replace it at the end of break without Mr L even noticing. This was a long shot, and he couldn't imagine what might happen if he were caught, but whatever it was would be better than what would happen if that duct tape never found its way into the right hands.

He edged the door open. Mr L held up a finger to say he was busy as he continued talking on the phone. Charlie inched toward the desk.

By some marvelous stroke of luck, Mr L had used the duct tape that morning to repair the binding on Albert's math book. It hadn't been replaced in the drawer and now sat on the corner of the desk.

Charlie reached this corner then stood, trembling, waiting for Mr L to finish. Mr L gave him a look as if to say he should go back out to break. Charlie shook his head no. Mr L covered the phone with one hand and turned.

"Charlie, what is it? Can't you see I'm busy?"

"Please sir, I need the homework for Thursday, now!"

"No, you do not. And my patience is about up with you. If you don't get outside and play, I will triple your homework for tonight and every other day of the week!"

Mr L swiveled back around and Charlie wasted no time running out of the classroom. Mr L had snapped at him. He had gotten in minor trouble. He felt terrible. But the duct tape was in his hand.

A cry of triumph came from around the corner of the building. Charlie deposited the stolen goods in Jake's outstretched hand then watched him run toward the woods. Not knowing what else to do, Charlie followed.

By the time Charlie arrived at the edge of the pit, Jake was already deep in the mud with the crowd. Timmy lifted both his hands and there was a pause, followed by an enormous cheer; apparently the duct tape worked. In the desperate scramble that followed, Charlie only picked out bits of what went on, but it appeared that the fifth graders were furiously refilling the hole with the heaps of dirt that had been piled up on either side, as Leo shouted orders from above.

Charlie stepped away from the chaos of flying dirt and flailing shovels. Then loud and clear he heard Porge at his side.

"Break's being called! Back to class! Two minute warning!"

There was a massive stampede as the fifth graders buried their shovels and emerged from the hole— which Charlie was amazed to see had almost been halfway refilled— then gathered at the edge of the wood to walk out in pairs of two, so as not to arouse suspicion. Leo instructed those waiting to scrape themselves on the trunks of nearby trees and roll around in the grass and pine needles to clean off the worst of the dirt. The scene reminded Charlie of one he saw recently in a black and white war movie, before his mother had made him go to bed because of the violence. He quickly ducked out and rushed back to class.

Mr L was waiting outside the classroom. He locked eyes with Charlie and beckoned him over. Charlie's entire stomach sank to his shoes. He felt his face grow hot. Mr L did not look happy.

"Charlie," he said, when Charlie was in front of him, "I have a question for you."

"Yessir?" Charlie mumbled.

"Where is the duct tape that was on my desk?"

Charlie looked frantically around. Fifth graders were lining up, straggling in from the field, happily chatting and jostling as if nothing had gone wrong.

"Look at me, Charlie," said Mr L. "I want to know where the duct tape went. When I was at my desk earlier it was there, then somehow after you came and asked that question about homework, it was gone."

"I d- d- don't—" Charlie stammered.

"Look at me," Mr L repeated, slowly. "Where is the duct tape?"

Charlie began to cave. His lower lip trembled. It was too much. Then he burst out:

"I'm sorry Mr L, it's not my fault but I took—"

The rest of Charlie's answer was lost in a shrill scream from the back of the line. Mr L darted over to find Porge crumpled on the ground, clutching his ankle, screaming about pain.

A quick survey of the wound determined there was nothing wrong. Porge insisted he had twisted it and it hurt like hundreds of prickly needles every time he stepped on it, but Mr L said that with a bit of walking around he would be fine. Amazingly, he was. He happily thanked Mr L, who sighed and returned to Charlie, just as Jake was slipping unnoticed out of the classroom.

"I'll deal with you later, Charlie," Mr L said. "Now we have to start class. Come in and—"

He stopped at the door. There, next to the desk where it had clearly been knocked to the floor, was the duct tape. Mr L felt a surge of remorse.

"I'm so sorry, Charlie," he said as he welcomed Charlie into the classroom. "I must've knocked the duct tape on

62

the floor myself. I shouldn't have accused you of it."

"No, sir, that's fine—"

"And look at you! You're covered in dirt! You ended up having a fun break after all." Mr L beamed. "I'm proud of you, Charlie. Don't worry, I'll get that Thursday homework to you after class, I promise."

Charlie forgot to stay after class to get the Thursday homework. Mr L had said that everyone was so well-behaved that day, that as a reward there would be no homework that night. Everyone left eagerly and excited for the afternoon, chattering about what they would do with all their newfound free time, and with a slow, pensive step, Charlie followed. He had a headache and desperately needed a nap.

8

SNAPPY THE TURTLE

During first break on Wednesday, Greg stumbled upon a turtle. He found it near the fence on the side of the field that dropped down through the woods into a creek, beyond the boundaries of the school. He proudly showed it to everyone during Natural History class, explaining how he had located it using his superior hunting and trapping skills. Then he named the turtle Snappy.

"It's not even a snapping turtle," Timmy complained to Leo. "It's a box turtle."

Snappy was given a prominent terrarium in the window of the science room. Inside that room were all the class pets and nature experiments. Greg took Snappy out every break to show other boys how Snappy could race against other turtles, how if you shook him real fast he would disappear inside his shell, how you could then flip the shell upside down and spin it to get him to stick his head out again when it stopped, and other exciting displays of Greg's nature knowledge.

"We have to free Snappy," said Timmy, watching this turtle abuse with mounting anger. "Greg's gonna kill him."

"Who knows what Snappy's life was like in the wild," Leo said in response. "Maybe he had to deal with worse predators. Hawks, snakes, foxes— now all Snappy has to put up with is a ten year old boy yelling and poking his head. He's got food and a warm tank. That's not so bad."

"Snappy belongs in the wild," said Timmy flatly.

"Snappy is a clever turtle," Leo said. "He understands when it's necessary to make compromises."

"Greg is being so annoying about it."

Leo considered this.

"Let's set that turtle free."

"Okay, we can go to the nature room during lunch and take him out," said Timmy. "If we put him down at the edge of the woods, he'll find his way home."

"No," said Leo, "no, that won't work at all. If we want to do this, we've got to do what's best for Snappy. We've got to do it right."

That afternoon Timmy went to Leo's house, where they spent two hours crafting messages using cut-out letters from Leo's sister's old copies of Teen Vogue. The next day before school a crowd gathered around the door to the nature room. Greg pushed his way to the front to see.

"UR IN OVR UR HEAD. TERIBEL THNGS WIL

HAPN IF SNAPPY NOT FREE. U R WARND."

Beneath the glued-on lines of letters was a dark smudge, with five claw-shaped points.

"That's the signature," said one of the onlookers.

"It's a turtle!" said another.

Greg ripped the note off the door and held it up over his head.

"Someone thinks they can threaten me," he announced, "and this is what I say to that!"

He tore up the paper into many little pieces. Cheers sounded all around him.

"Snappy is mine," Greg said, "and Snappy will stay mine forever."

He marched off to class. Timmy looked to Leo.

"Well that backfired," he said.

"Not at all," said Leo. "This is why we made more than one sign."

After lunch there was a larger crowd gathered at the door to the nature room. A new sign read:

"RELESE SNAPPY OR WE TAK AKSHUN."

"Gentlemen," Greg cried, lifting the note high for all to see. "We do not negotiate with terrorists!"

He shredded this paper just like the last, and then instituted a 24-hour guard around Snappy's terrarium during school hours. Word spread and general interest in Snappy increased; groups of wide-eyed third graders gathered at the window of the nature room to watch Greg pace back and forth around Snappy's tank.

The next morning, sure enough there was a fresh sign

at the door.

"TODAY WE STRIK. 2ND BREK. UNLES SNAPPY FREE."

Greg laughed loudly, confident this was an empty threat. But nonetheless there was a steady clamor, especially among the third graders, asking for verification that they were in fact not in danger. Greg said terrorists were too afraid to attack the school because he was watching Snappy. This did not seem to comfort them. In fact, it had the opposite effect.

"They're going to blow up the school?" squealed a voice at the back of the group.

"I say we release Snappy!" cried another. "Before Greg gets us all killed over a turtle!"

The crowd agreed. The third graders started chanting for Snappy's release.

"You can't be serious," Greg bellowed. "That is exactly what the terrorists want!"

"We know," said a third grader. "That's why we're giving up Snappy, stupid!"

"Yeah!"

"Let him go!"

The crowd was on the verge of becoming a mob. Greg sensed he was losing them, but he did not intend to lose Snappy too.

"Listen," he said, leaping onto the wooden bench outside the nature room, "what we have here is a threat to our freedom as a country and as a people. These terrorists are bullies who think they can threaten us and get whatever they want. They think we are weak. Well, I say no. We are strong. And even if it takes blowing up this entire school and killing every last one of us, I say we keep Snappy!"

In fairness to Greg, most boys were on his side until the last sentence of his speech. After that, he had pretty much turned even those who were sympathetic with holding onto the turtle, or at least apathetic with regards to the whole situation, into supporters of the "Release Snappy" party. Greg saw this and took a different tactic. He sprinted into the nature room and locked the door after him. There was loud banging and screaming as the frenzied third graders attempted entrance. Then morning class was called.

Before second break, apart from standard classes, there would be first break and lunch. Greg knew he had to defend Snappy at those times if he wanted his position to last. So, sure enough, as soon as they were released for first break he sprinted out of the classroom and over to the nature room.

But the third graders had gotten there first. Already a little pudgy hand was reaching for Snappy, while its owner's friends kept watch. They saw Greg coming and began to scream. It was too late.

The third graders were soundly defeated and Greg stood as guard once again over his controversial pet. All break there were rallies and protests outside the nature room. Leo probably did not help Greg's position by affirming the "Keep Snappy Safe" party and chanting loudly about how the destruction of the school would be but a small price to pay for one innocent turtle's safety. Greg was grateful for his efforts but not so much their effect, which seemed to double the crowd's fervor against the poor turtle.

"We don't know what the terrorists plan to do to Snappy!" Leo cried out, "To release him now could mean death! What has Snappy ever done to you?"

Such rhetoric unfortunately inspired no sympathy in the crowd, which struck up a new chant of "Death to Snappy! Death to Snappy!"

"This is getting out of hand," Timmy whispered to Leo, when break was almost over, and the onlookers began to realize they had a mere few hours left to live, should that turtle remain locked in its terrarium with Greg standing guard.

"Don't worry," Leo assured him; "it's almost time for our final phase."

After lunch was second break. Hardly any of the third graders could eat. They rushed straight to the nature room to get Snappy out at all costs, when they found a new sign on the door:

"30 MINUTS."

Then they discovered that Greg had stolen the key to the nature room and locked it from the outside. The chaos that ensued was interrupted by the arrival of Leo, out of breath, coming from the direction of the woods.

"I've changed my mind," he screamed. "Someone get Snappy. Get him out of there!"

"What happened?" asked a third grader, knowing Leo had been a fervent proponent of "Keep Snappy Safe." There was general confusion, and no little amount of dread, as they saw the terror in Leo's face.

"I thought it was all some stupid lie," he said, and now Greg, who had come from lunch, was listening too. "But then I went out with Timmy to play ninja in the woods—"

"We aren't allowed in the woods," said a third grader.

"And there's good reason for that," Leo said darkly, "good reason which I now understand."

"What happened?" said a voice from the back.

"After I saw them I ran as fast as I could back here. And then Timmy— wait where's Timmy? Timmy?"

"Stop!" said Greg, jumping forward to grab Leo's shoulders, turning him away from the woods and back to him. "Pull yourself together! Who was in the woods?"

"Big men in strange suits carrying guns," stammered Leo. "They had some giant metal case, talking about saving a turtle, taking revenge and blowing up the— where's Timmy? Have you seen Timmy?"

"The terrorists have Timmy!" screamed a third grader.

"They've got a bomb!"

"Give them Snappy!"

"We're running out of time!"

This last sentence was yelled by Greg himself, on whom the gravity of the situation had fallen at last. Unfortunately, as he pulled at the door handle, he remembered he had locked the door and not only that— he'd forgotten where he'd put the key.

"I think," he hesitated, "I think maybe it's in my cubby. No maybe the lunchroom."

"We have fifteen minutes!" shrieked a third grader.

"And that's counting from when you read the sign," Leo pointed out. "Who knows how long it's been since they put it up."

Greg couldn't waste another second thinking about the key. He picked up the wooden bench and shoved it through the window, spraying glass everywhere, pushing the terrarium off the ledge to where it shattered on the floor. There was a general gasp; but then they saw, in the heap of jagged shards, a small shell. Snappy was safe.

Greg reached in, carefully, and picked up the shell. He only got three scratches on his arm, none of which were that deep. Then he held Snappy aloft, to a chorus of cheers, and sprinted across the field to the woods.

Once there the crowd stopped, peering into the seemingly innocent spaces among the trees. Any of them could be hiding strangers who plotted to blow up everything they held dear.

"Here," Greg yelled, "we give you Snappy!"

He placed the turtle on the ground. Nothing happened.

"Make him go in the woods," said a third grader.

"It's not enough, that turtle's so slow, they won't get him in time!"

"Someone's gotta take him in!"

"I'll take him," said a brave voice from the back.

Leo stepped forward. He scooped Snappy up in one hand, and patted Greg's shoulder with the other.

"Whatever happens, Greg," he said, "I forgive you."

Then he walked off into the woods. Most of the crowd were convinced they would never see him again. Indeed they stood staring into the trees for nearly ten whole minutes. That's how long it took for Leo to find Timmy, hop the fence, then jog down to the creek where they put Snappy nice and safe on a large wet rock.

When Leo reemerged with no Snappy and one Timmy, the crowd went wild. He was hailed as a hero and carried back to the classrooms. No boy now had even the slightest worry that the threat of destruction would be carried out. They believed they were safe. And they were right.

Greg was soundly punished for destruction of school property. He figured the price of the window repairs and the ensuing detentions were but a small sacrifice for the survival and wellbeing of his entire school. Unfortunately, the teachers had not applauded his bravery in returning Snappy to the wild. Nor had they been impressed with Leo's behavior; this was not the first time Leo had been punished for spreading panic.

Timmy, however, observed Greg's forfeited breaks and detentions after school with a smile. Snappy had been vindicated. Somehow, it seemed Leo always knew the right thing to do.

9

TRENCH WARFARE

On Monday the boys noticed a change in their recess space. The grassy area on one side of the field had been suddenly covered by mounds and mounds of new black dirt and fresh wood chips. Mr L explained that this space was being used as a holdover site for construction that was going on at another part of the school, and would most likely be there the whole week. Someone asked if they could play in it. Mr L paused, then shrugged and said that was fine, as long as they didn't make too much of a mess.

Wednesday, 13:05. Leo leaned against the wall of black dirt behind him, chest heaving. How had it come to this? Timmy, who was craning his neck to look out over the wall, announced that Porge was coming. Thank God.

Porge dove into the trench and thrust himself back

against the wall. He was covered in dirt and had scratches up both arms.

"Well? Well?" demanded Leo, "What happened?"

"They got him," Porge gasped for breath. "They got Jake."

Leo swore. Not a very bad word, but bad enough to not print it here. Timmy glanced from his look-out to his leader, then back.

"Grenade!" he screamed.

A pinecone bounced against the back wall and fell in the dirt at Leo's feet. Porge jumped up and kicked it down the winding trench, out of view.

"Good work, lieutenant," said Leo, "that was close. What's it look like out there?"

"Getting worse," Timmy said. "They're preparing another attack."

"Of course they are," muttered Leo. "Now that Jake's captured, what's stopping them? How many?"

"Hard to tell, captain. Looks like they've built an outpost in no man's land."

Leo looked to Porge for confirmation. Porge nodded.

"Not only that," Porge said with a cough, still fighting for breath, "but they've been talking to fourth graders."

"Fourth graders!" Leo said, "Greg's already got the entire third grade fighting for him!"

"He wants more. Offers them candy from home and other bribes. They're still holding out, but who knows for how long?"

"The fourth grade is supposed to be neutral!"

Leo kicked the wall, angry at the injustice of the world and fickleness of men's hearts. Then he scrabbled up to peer over the edge, positioning himself next to Timmy.

The barren space of trampled dirt extended before him beneath a pale and uncaring sky. Somewhere a bird started to sing. That nature could still thrive in a world that contained such desolation, Leo could not imagine. But he hadn't the luxury to dwell on such thoughts.

"Show me where the grenade came from," he said.

Timmy pointed. There was a small lump of dirt not twenty feet away. Beyond it at a slight rise Leo could see the jagged line of the enemy's trench.

"They've dug in," he noted, "and are expanding."

"So are we," said Timmy, nodding to his left. Around the bend in their dugout Jeffrey and Albert were furiously carving out a space for retreat. Leo glanced in their direction with a slight frown. He didn't want to go backwards and give up ground. But sometimes it was necessary to dig in and wait, wait for the chance to strike.

All the same, this entire war had been waiting. Day after day of making no progress, fighting for entire breaks over a mere ten yards. But soon, he could feel it, soon the tide would turn. Soon, but not now. Not now that Jake was somewhere over there, captured, held at the mercy of the enemy.

Leo jogged round the bend in the trench and ducked below the surface, feeling his way along and down until he could only go forward on his knees. Light was sparse down here, but he could see two pairs of feet jutting from a deeper hole, from which dirt was flying backward.

"Well?" he said. "How's it coming?"

"Slow," a voice groaned.

"Albert," Leo addressed the owner of the voice, "we're going to need you at the front. The third graders are preparing an attack and we need numbers."

"Oh sweet relief," said Albert, quickly abandoning his digging stick. He wriggled past Leo and crawled out to the open of the outer trenches, gulping fresh air.

"How about you," Leo said to the other digger, "you want to fight?"

"Oh, no, that's okay," said Jeffrey, turning to squint at Leo. His entire face and hair were covered in dirt, so that Leo could only see the whites of his eyes and teeth. Leo shuddered. War was a terrible thing.

"I'll keep digging," Jeffrey went on, "we need the retreat hole in case you guys can't hold them off. We propped up that piece of wood like you said, up near the entrance to the trenches, so we can block the hole if they invade."

"Good," Leo nodded, "let's hope that never happens."

He turned to wriggle back to the trench.

"Leo, wait," said Jeffrey. "Be careful up there."

"I'll try," said Leo, "but it's hard to be careful in the middle of hell."

With that gem of wisdom he slid back up to the outer world.

"Leo!" Timmy screamed, as he jogged around the bend. "It's happening! Now!"

Leo grit his teeth and pulled himself up to risk a glance over the trench. Filthy third graders climbed out of the opposite holes like an army of the undead emerging from their graves, screeching a hideous war cry. At their front was Greg, shirt tied over his head, bare chest smeared with dirt, lifting his war stick high in the air and hollering.

"What are you waiting for?" Leo said to his troops. "Fire back!"

"If we attack they'll know where we are!" Albert howled.

"They'll know soon enough anyway! Fire!"

At Leo's command Porge and Albert took to the ammunition stores, heaving a barrage of acorns and pinecones at the charging army. Third graders were hit, some fell, others stumbled, but it wasn't enough. There were too many.

"Dirt!" Leo commanded. "They're close enough, switch to dirt!"

Timmy uncovered the next store of ammunition and now they flung heavy balls of dirt over the wall at the attacking army. This was met with cries of anguish and confusion, as many third graders tried to run back, colliding with those coming forward.

"To the ground!" Greg's loud voice was heard over the screaming. "Take to the ground!"

He flung himself on his belly and began to crawl forward. His army followed and the dirt clods flew overhead. Leo held up his hand then waited, digging his foot halfway up the wall of the trench, and his soldiers did likewise.

"Now!" he screamed suddenly. "Charge!"

The suddenness of the counter-attack served its purpose. Leo, Timmy, Albert, and Porge rushed onto no man's land and before Greg and his army knew what was happening, they had struck. The third graders hardly had time to switch from their bellies to their knees.

Leo and his noble army kicked dirt in their attackers' faces and wrestled them back to the ground, yelling for them to call uncle and surrender. Third graders squealed and scattered, retreating like a herd of startled piglets. But Greg continued to thrash and fight. Having regained his feet, he grappled with Leo in the middle of the battlefield. He would not retreat, not yet.

Leo soon saw why. Greg pushed off him and howled like a wolf, making a signal for his army. The scattering third graders heard this and looked to their left. Leo looked too, as did his army.

"Aw man, no fair," moaned Albert.

An entire squadron of fourth graders charged the dirt, returning Greg's howl. They sprinted straight at Leo and the others, hurling acorns, fresh and ready for blood. Leo had no choice but to call the retreat.

He and his soldiers dove back into the trench as the oncoming armies joined and charged together, the reinvigorated third graders along with the clean-faced fourth graders, led by the impervious Greg.

Leo's forces hurled dirt in droves, but it wasn't enough. The attackers spilled over the walls and through the trench like a raging flood, kicking dirt and destroying walls, grasping for captives.

"Retreat!" Leo cried out, grabbing his soldiers and pulling them back. "Retreat!"

In the chaos of the invasion they slipped around the corner and crawled down the retreat hole into the hidden trench. Albert scrambled round and kicked at the wooden support board until it gave way; the ceiling of the exit passage collapsed and blocked them in.

"Great," said Porge, "now we're stuck."

"Ow, that's my face," groaned Albert. "Move your foot."

"Shush," Leo hissed. "Don't let them hear you."

They waited many long moments for the frenzied cries to die down. Someone announced the trench had been abandoned; this was followed by a rousing cheer.

"Okay listen," Leo whispered, "we can't be in here long."

"Yeah, because we'd die," Albert said. "There's no air."

"I made little air holes," came a cheerful voice from further down; "I've needed them, since I've been here all break."

"But you had air coming from the passage too, Jeffrey," said Leo, "the passage we just blocked. Albert's right, there's not much time before we all suffocate."

Porge began yelping and wildly digging at the wall, so that Timmy and Albert had to hold him down.

"Pull yourself together, private," Leo snapped; "this is war, we don't have the luxury to panic. I'm thinking of a plan. Before we do anything, we have to lie low and wait. Give them a false sense of security. Our strongest weapon is surprise."

As he said this they heard footsteps above them. Leo shut his eyes as trails of dirt descended from the ceiling. He had faith in Jeffrey, but all the same, there was doubt that the hole would stand.

"They're hiding in the woods," came the loud voice of their opposing general, directly above them. "Bunch of fraidy-cats. But if I know Leo, he's working out some dumb plan right now to attack and try to take back their land. Freddy, listen up."

"Yes, Greg, sir!" said a small voice that belonged to the leader of the third graders.

"I want your grunts to reinforce the backside of the trenches. Prepare for an attack from the woods. Got it?"

"Very good, Greg, sir!"

"Maurice, take a team of your best fourth graders and scout around the trees. If you see the enemy, do not engage, but report back at once. Got it? We've got most of our numbers in this trench. This is where the battle's going to be. And Freddy, make sure we keep a twenty-four hour watch on The Berserker."

"There are seven good men watching him right now, Greg, sir!"

"They're third graders, not men. Remember that. Alright, soldiers, we have won the battle, but not the war. Be prepared for anything."

"Sir, yes, Greg, sir!" said two voices in unison.

After the receding footsteps there was silence on the hump of dirt above them. But Leo kept quiet. He had only counted two pairs of feet walking away. Sure enough, a minute later, the voice yelled above them loud and clear.

"Oy! Maurice! Make sure you check the back corner over there! Those slugs could be anywhere!"

Greg was using the hump above them as a look-out point. Leo bit his lip. This could complicate things. Next to him, Porge was making muted gasping noises. They had to act, and fast.

"Jeffrey," Leo hissed, "how far to the surface, if you keep digging forward, and not up?"

"I believe we could break ground in about ten feet," he said, "but wouldn't Greg see?"

"Just start digging. Porge, pick up a stick. Feeling faint? Well dig. Dig like your life depends on it. Because it does."

The furious digging commenced. To Leo's relief, footsteps overhead indicated that Greg had walked down to the trench, probably to inspect the third graders' new fortifications.

A sliver of light penetrated the blackness. Porge gasped down air. Leo wriggled over to where they were and explained his plan. Porge nodded, then readied himself, digging stick clutched to his chest.

"Not you, Jeffrey," said Leo. "This time we need you for the fight."

Jeffrey followed him back into the heart of the retreat hole, as Leo, Timmy, and Albert crawled toward their occupied trench.

But just as they crouched, preparing to strike, they heard footsteps again on the hump of dirt above.

"Not anywhere in the woods? Are you kidding me? They're clearly hiding! Duh! Look in the trees, look in the piles of leaves! Yes! Go! Fourth graders. So much stupid."

Leo changed plans. He quickly whispered the new strategy to each soldier in the hole. Then, he gave the signal to Porge.

"Now!" he yelled, and together they thrust their digging sticks into the ceiling, standing up as they did so. The dirt collapsed on top of them, and with it, a very surprised Greg.

Waving sticks and flailing limbs, unearthing themselves was difficult work, but the soldiers fought valiantly. They had surprise on their side; the third and fourth graders in the trenches stood and gaped as Leo's army emerged, dragging Greg down as they went.

After overcoming his shock Greg began to fight back, but by that time Leo had pulled himself free and yanked Timmy up with him. Albert came next, but Jeffrey was still half-buried. Instead of pulling himself up further, he latched on to Greg and would not release his grip, no matter how much Greg yelled and struggled and called him names. With the enemy's leader thus incapacitated, Leo, Timmy, and Albert charged at the hoards that occupied their base.

At first, all but the bravest of third graders ran from these dirt-covered marauders, who had burst up from the dirt like horrible subterranean man-beasts. But the fourth graders closed in behind, plugging the trench, and the third graders were forced to turn and fight. Leo and his soldiers mowed them down with a ravenous fury, sending bodies ricocheting off the walls, throwing the smaller boys into the dirt, or even tossing them out of the trench. But the fourth graders at the back pressed further forward, creating a bottle-neck pressure point at the center. Here Greg's army refused to budge, their impassable strength given by sheer force of numbers.

"Can't get through!" Albert screamed, as he attempted to plunge into the writhing mass of third graders.

"Pull them away!" screamed Leo, and he began yanking the third graders free and throwing them on the ground behind him, but it wasn't enough; they rose again and soon the brave warriors were hemmed in on both sides, trapped.

The surprise of the assault was over, the third graders had regained their fighting zeal, and to make matters worse, the other squad of fourth graders returned from the woods with a storm of howls. They reinforced the other side of the line and pushed.

"Stay on your feet," Leo cried over the roar, propping Timmy up. "Don't fall you'll be trampled!"

"Don't, know, if I, can hold," stammered Timmy, trying to breathe.

"Just a little more," urged Leo.

Then a loud laugh came from directly overhead. There stood Greg, hands on hips, watching the struggle in the trench.

"Well, well, well," he sneered, "caught like skunks in a trap."

"Come fight you wuss!" Albert screamed.

"In there? No way. I'll let my third grade army finish you off. How's it feel, Leo? To be beaten by a bunch of third graders?"

"Eat dirt, you poop!"

This last brave sentence came from behind Greg. Jeffrey had risen and now gave Greg a huge shove. It wasn't enough to push him off his feet, but it was enough to nudge him slightly from behind, nudge him just enough to trip down into the trench, right on top of Leo.

Leo grappled and the third graders seethed, but Greg was flailing wildly, and with his superior numbers he would've soon pinned Leo and his two soldiers. Unable to bear the sight, Jeffrey tore his gaze away from the carnage below and lifted his eyes to no man's land. Then hope broke over his features, radiant like the spreading sun at dawn, and he smiled.

"Leo," he said softly, "he's coming."

There, sprinting across the field and leaving moaning, fallen third graders in his wake, was Jake the Berserker. Right behind him was Porge, who had snuck around the field to come back and liberate their strongest weapon. As Jake neared he began to scream, his signature eerie shriek that gave him his title. The third graders heard this and froze. Blood ran cold in their veins. They turned, struggled to get out of the trench, to get away, to get anywhere that was not there, but the fourth graders still hemmed them in. Jake leapt into the fray.

Third graders flew through the air like shovelfuls of dirt, as Jake plowed his way through the trench. The unlucky ones were picked up and heaved, while others threw themselves on the ground and groveled before the Berserker, begging for mercy. Jake easily carved a hole in the squirming masses, as Porge jumped in behind and took on the fourth graders, now with the help of Albert and Timmy, while Greg looked on in horror. Then Jake turned, enraged, and began to run straight at Greg, who was being held by Leo.

Greg twisted and kneed Leo in the stomach, hard, then stepped on him on his way out of the trench. Jake dove but missed; Greg was already sprinting back to his own trench, yelling for retreat.

The remaining third and fourth graders fled after Greg, back to the safety of their holes. They dragged their own injured and stragglers, as Albert and Porge walked the length of the trench, lifting the bodies of the fallen and rolling them back onto no man's land, where they crawled to their feet, groaning and complaining as they stumbled back to their side.

Leo leaned against the wall, clutching his stomach. Silence fell in the trench. Jake stood nearby, covered with scratches, his hair tangled, eyes wild. Leo coughed and itched his skin, caked with dirt. They had survived the battle. But there would be another. And another. An entire day's worth of war, and what had been achieved? They held their position. But so did Greg.

He lifted himself to look over the edge of the trench, as the last of the wounded dropped out of sight into Greg's stronghold on the other side. Is this what man was, a beast to crawl in dirt and struggle with his fellow creatures? What was the point? When would it all end? Leo knew he had to think about the next plan, about the next battle. But he'd seen enough fighting. And soon it would all start up again, and it wouldn't stop until one side stamped out the other, forever.

The bird sang again. The sound was sweet to his ears, and as Leo paused to listen, he noticed again the cold blue sky. How could beauty exist in such a world?

He glanced back to his ragtag group of followers. His warriors, no, his brothers. There was Jake, still regaining his breath, rage not yet subsided. Albert sat in the dirt, moaning. Timmy and Porge stood at attention, waiting for their next command, though Leo could see how fatigued they were. Porge could barely stand straight. And Jeffrey was digging. Always digging.

Leo brought himself to full height, and pounded his palm with his fist. They had won this fight and they would win the war. They would never stop this struggle until the enemy had been conquered, they would—

The bell rang. Teachers called for line-up. The boys scrambled out of the hole and brushed dirt off their clothes as they jogged back to class. Break was over.

10

MR L GETS PRANKED

"And that is why photosynthesis is the most important biological function of a plant."

"Mr L?"

"Yes, Timmy?"

"I still don't understand, could you draw a picture please?"

"Of course, Timmy."

Mr L happily walked to the board, pleased that his student was interested enough to want a diagram of photosynthesis. As he scanned the classroom, it seemed that more than the usual faces were eagerly watching him reach for the color-coded markers. This encouraged him even more.

"See a plant cell, which we'll draw in green, looks like this…"

He paused. The line that he'd drawn was purple. He examined the marker, which had a green cap. A smattering of giggles broke out in his audience.

"Whoops," he said, "must've switched the caps by accident."

He reached for the marker with the purple cap, then tried it on the board. The result was orange.

The giggles grew into unrestrained laughter.

"Did you guys switch the caps on me?" said Mr L, with a good-natured smile.

The boys nodded, and Mr L proceeded to try the other markers as they laughed even harder. Finally, he was able to replace the caps to their proper markers.

"Alright," he said, "you got me."

"We sure did!" said Jeffrey.

All the boys laughed. All the boys, that is, except Greg. He looked around the room and frowned.

After lunch that same day, Mr L read from the history book. They were learning about the Native American tradition of planting corn. Greg was drawing a very detailed depiction of a stick figure getting scalped after trying to steal an ear of corn, when he noticed movement out of the corner of his eye. Mr L finished reading the page and looked up.

"Okay, why don't you continue reading, Jake?" he said.

But he looked straight at Porge.

"I'm sorry," said Porge, "did you mean me?"

A wave of giggles swept the classroom. Mr L blinked.

"Sorry, I thought you were—" he said, then smiled

knowingly. "Ah," he said, "you and Jake switched places didn't you?"

Laughter erupted throughout the classroom.

"They did!" squealed Jeffrey. "They switched places when you weren't looking!"

"Alright, you can switch back now," Mr L said, "you little tricksters."

"That was a sweet prank," said Albert to Jake, high-fiving him as he resumed his seat.

"Looks like it's the day of pranks, huh?" said Mr L as everyone continued to laugh. "Well let's get back to corn…"

Greg was no longer interested in his picture. He glared at his classmates with evident disdain. That was their idea of a prank?

"Hey, hey Jake," he said during second break, "I have a great idea for a prank on Mr L."

But Jake wasn't listening. He had his head together with Porge and Timmy and they were planning on switching the bookmarks in Mr L's text books, so that when he opened them to teach, he'd be in a different spot from when he left off. This was more adventurous than their previous attempts, but if Mr L didn't notice and just read whatever page he opened to, they felt it would all be worth it.

"We'll totally get him," giggled Porge.

"Everyone will laugh!" said Timmy.

"I'll do the switching," said Jake confidently. "He'll never even notice."

"Hey, Porge," said Greg, "I got a great prank for—"

"Quiet Greg, we're planning something important," said Porge, and the three pranksters moved away.

"Oh boy," said Jeffrey, coming up next to Greg and looking with admiration at his fellow classmates. "I wonder what those guys are going to come up with next!"

"Probably something dumb," snorted Greg.

"Are you kidding?" Jeffrey said. "I mean, switching places when Mr L wasn't looking? They've got nerve."

"Jeffrey, listen, I have an awesome idea for a prank. During lunch tomorrow—"

But Jeffrey was already walking away, chuckling to himself. Greg looked around, frustrated. Charlie was doing his homework next to the classroom door.

"Hey, Charlie," he said, "want to pull a prank on Mr L with me?"

Charlie snapped his book shut and sprinted away. He was already partially scandalized by what had happened that day, and wanted nothing to do with whatever Greg was planning.

"Sorry Greg," said Albert behind him, "you gotta leave the real pranking to the pranksters."

"You call those pranks?" Greg snapped, "those were the lamest—"

"Sounds like someone's jealous," Albert interrupted, with a knowing smile.

"Jealous? Listen, Albert, I have a prank that's so cool none of those guys are even—"

"Sure you do," said Albert, patting Greg on the

shoulder, "sure you do."

He walked away as Greg stood and seethed. He decided he would prank Mr L himself. Then they'd all see.

The next day after lunch, Mr L opened the history book again:

"And that is why the Nina, the Pinta, and the— hey, didn't we read this part already?"

"We did! We read that on Tuesday!" Jeffrey screamed with glee.

"Someone must've switched my bookmark," exclaimed Mr L, "just like what happened during math!"

The class broke into laughter. Jeffrey laughed so hard he fell out of his desk. Jake and Timmy high-fived. Greg was silent.

"Oh man, you guys are silly this week," said Mr L, shaking his head.

"We sure are!" giggled Jeffrey.

"Well, let's get back to the right page. Does anyone remember…"

"Page fifty-six," said Charlie.

"Alright," Mr L said, turning his pages, "so here we are, still on corn. The Native Americans—"

With an enormous THUD, Mr L's head hit the desk.

There was a moment of stunned silence. No one moved. Mr L was completely still.

"Hah!" Greg yelled, jumping out of his desk and pointing at the unconscious teacher. "You got pranked!"

He reached over to high-five Jake, but his hand hung

unregarded in the air. No one moved or spoke. Everyone was looking at Mr L, who was slumped motionless on the desk. Both his hands hung down to the floor, his cheek pressed against the history book, and a little pool of drool gathered over the picture of corn.

"I did it!" Greg tried again, "look guys, I got him good!"

"What did you do?" said Porge in horror.

"Is he d- d- dead?" stammered Jeffrey, sniffing back a tear.

"No, idiot, he's just drugged," Greg said confidently. "I snuck some of my mom's dissolving sleeping pills into his water bottle during lunch. Shook it up and he didn't even notice. Gave him a double dose so he'll be out for a long time."

This explanation of his cleverness did not have the effect he desired on the class. They continued to stare from him to Mr L with open mouths.

"See," he said, looking around in defiance, "that's a real prank."

"So you poisoned him," Leo said at last. "You poisoned the teacher. Greg, do you know how illegal that is?"

"Probably just as illegal as switching the caps on markers," Greg snorted, then paused. "Okay maybe a little bit more illegal, but only because it's way cooler. Anyway that's not important!"

He ran to the front of the classroom, looking all around.

"Don't you guys understand? We have the whole day free, because Mr L is asleep! We can scream and yell and he'll do nothing! We can have break for the rest of the day! No school at all! Best prank ever!"

Even Albert, who might've in another circumstance welcomed such news with tears of joy, understood that the current situation was not to be celebrated.

"Sit down!" Charlie shrieked from the back of the room, overcoming his initial shock. "Mr M is walking by! If he sees you he'll come in and check what's going on!"

Everyone, even Greg, understood immediately that the last thing they wanted was another teacher entering the room. Greg dove back in his chair as Mr M walked past the window, casually glancing in and giving a wave to Mr L. The boys looked at one another.

A second later Mr M appeared again, concern on his face. He put his face up to the glass and peered through. But there was Mr L, sitting up and nodding back at him. Mr L returned his wave with a casual flick of his hand. Mr M smiled and walked on.

"Don't move," Leo said to Timmy and Jake, who were behind Mr L's chair propping him up by the torso. Jake held Mr L's head up by his hair and controlled his arm with his other hand.

"He might come back," said Leo.

"He's just going to the faculty room for coffee," Charlie whispered, "so everyone keep your books open. Make it look like you're working."

Sure enough, three minutes later Mr M walked back,

mug of coffee in hand. He barely nodded toward the classroom this time, confident that all was well.

"That was close," said Jeffrey.

"My arms are tired," said Timmy.

"Okay," said Leo, standing up. "We have to think of what to do."

"We can do whatever we want!" Greg insisted, "because we pranked Mr L and—"

"*We* didn't do anything," Jeffrey squealed. "*You* tried to kill him! This is attempted murder!"

"I didn't kill anyone," snorted Greg.

"What Greg did," said Leo, "is certainly punishable in court. He will go to jail. But when the police come to examine Mr L, they're going to look for accomplices. That's what happens when you prosecute crimes. And we have all participated in pranks in this classroom so—"

"Not me," interrupted Charlie.

"So we will *all* be punished," Leo finished, frowning at Charlie.

Panic took hold of the class. Albert made a dive for Greg, who began wrestling with him. Jeffrey starting screaming that he needed his lawyer. Timmy insisted again that his arms were tired.

"Cut it out!" said Leo loudly, commanding their attention. "If we make a scene then another teacher will come in. Quiet!"

"They'll come and they'll think it's funny," explained Greg, "just like Mr L when he wakes up. Because it's a prank!"

Everyone glared at Greg. Leo was almost out of patience.

"Listen up," he snarled, "you got us into this mess. And you better help us out of it. If this goes to the police it's on you. Do you realize that? You drugged a teacher! You think they'll let you just walk away?"

"You mean, I'd be kicked out of school?" said Greg. As much as he liked to gripe about school, he did enjoy it.

"You'll be kicked out of society! Is there a school in prison on some banished island somewhere? I don't know, Greg, because I've never been. I've never drugged a teacher before. But you'll find out soon enough, you'll know all about prisons on empty islands where crazy, dangerous people get sent, because that's where you'll be, Greg!"

"That's where we'll all be," said Jeffrey quietly, with a shiver.

Charlie suddenly made a run for the door.

"Stop him!" Leo bellowed.

Porge and Albert sprang up to hold him back.

"I'm, going, to, tell," Charlie stuttered, as he struggled to get through. "Mr L, might need, medical, attention—"

"He's breathing just fine," Jake called out from behind the chair. "It's Timmy who needs medical attention."

"He's so heavy!" cried Timmy. "My arms!"

"Charlie, pull yourself together," snapped Leo. "You are in this class and you have to act like it. No one gets out of this. And Jeffrey, no one is going to prison. Not even Greg. Because here's what we're going to do. Jake, listen closely. In Mr L's drawer is a roll of duct tape…"

When Mr M passed again, twenty minutes later, he saw all of Mr L's class hard at work taking notes from their History books. Mr L sat up in his chair and watched them. Mr M was impressed at how he kept his students in such careful control.

As they pretended to take notes at their desks, Leo talked with Charlie to devise a strategy. The best way to mitigate the potential catastrophe that would arise from an outside party discovering the drugged teacher would be to proceed as if nothing had happened. Each class went by, directed by Charlie from his desk, and every student diligently took notes and did their work as in any other day.

Grammar worksheets were completed and stacked nicely in the "submitted work" tray. Charlie led two spelling exercises and then explained a writing assignment he found in Mr L's lesson book for that day. This completed assignment was also placed in the "submitted work" tray.

Second break posed a difficulty, as teachers often came in to chat with Mr L while the classroom was vacated. It was Greg, now completely committed to upholding the appearance of a harmonious classroom, who had the idea to stage a punishment session. The line "I will not talk back to the teacher" was written on the board and Greg, Jake, Albert, and Leo sat in desks to industriously copy this line onto notebook paper as many times as they could. In addition, a "please do not disturb, punishment in progress" sign was taped to the door. Jeffrey and Charlie stood watch, dissuading any students or even teachers from going any farther. They shook their heads and said Mr L was in a mood; the class had been poorly behaved and he was not likely to be kind to any one who disturbed him now.

A couple third and fourth graders peeked in at the window, watching the naughty fifth graders being punished. Sure enough, there was angry Mr L, sitting up stiff and unmoving in his chair, watching those poor troublemakers copy lines. Break went without a hitch.

In the final two periods, Charlie taught the class Literature then an extra math lesson for good measure. He wrote the homework on the board and everyone copied it down. They straightened up the desks and cleaned the classroom, packing up quietly, before removing the duct tape and shifting Mr L to a comfortable position.

"No one mentions this," said Leo, "ever."

He switched off the lights and the class filed out. All in all, it was an oddly uneventful day.

Mr L woke up around 5:45. Stumbling to the light switch, he couldn't for the life of him remember what had happened. Then he saw the homework on the board. He'd assigned slightly more than usual, which was interesting, and apparently had asked Charlie to write it for everyone to copy down. Try as he might, he couldn't remember a single thing since lunch.

So he took out some of Albert's notebooks. Amazingly, there were all the notes for History, Grammar, and even

Literature. He saw that he had given them a math challenge problem and— incredibly— Albert had copied the problem into his math book! He'd even attempted to solve it!

Now Mr L was excited. He pulled out other notebooks; Porge, Timmy, Jeffrey, they were all the same. He had covered more material that day than any of the three days beforehand combined! Not only that, but there was a neat stack of papers ready to be graded in the "submitted work" tray. Along with that, there were punishments turned in from Leo, Greg, Jake, and Albert. Mr L couldn't help but smile. Even during such a productive afternoon, the usual suspects had managed to get in trouble.

What bothered him was that he still couldn't remember any of it. The best afternoon of his teaching career and he had no recollection— Mr L sat in his chair and thought. Of course, he must've been so into his lessons, so engaged in the material— he had even inspired Albert to learn, of all people— that he had completely exhausted himself. After school he must've flicked off the lights for a little nap, which was not unusual for Mr L, though such nap times were usually after very difficult teaching days. He would wake up from those necessary naps even more exhausted than before, remembering everything. But today he'd woken up completely refreshed, as if he'd slept deeply for hours. Mr L smiled. He felt nothing except a dull throb in his forehead; this must be the feeling of a job well done.

He packed up his books. The back of his neck itched,

and he realized that the hair there had disappeared. This was odd, he didn't remember shaving his neck. He must've done so over the weekend. Then he noticed something else and laughed out loud. His bookmark was still on the wrong page of the history book.

Thinking about his mischievous little students with an affectionate smile, he left the classroom and whistled on his way to his car. What a wonderful day he'd had. Sometimes he struggled to get his students to learn. But not today. Today, he had been the teacher he had always dreamed he would be. And man did it feel good.

11

EARTHWORM SALLY

The cult of Earthworm Sally was formally established on Wednesday, but by Friday it had made believers of nearly the entire fifth grade. High Priest Leo preached every break to a crowd of fervent worshippers and led the sacred rituals, as assisted by Archdeacon Timmy. The founding of this new and popular religion happened when the High Priest was excavating a mulch pile to expand his stick fort and found therein a worm that was four feet, seven inches long. Multiple rulers had been summoned from nearby classrooms to confirm the measurement.

This was no ordinary creature. The worm was elevated to a place of prominence in the fort, for it had not merely appeared; it had been sent. This was a prophet sent by the Great Ruler of the Deep, the fearful Earthworm Sally, who lived far beneath the earth in her dark lair, biding her time before she burst forth in rage and terror to wreak vengeance upon all nonbelievers. This humble fort was chosen, in the infinite mercy and compassion of Earthworm Sally, as a place where devotion might be shown so that at the reckoning of the world, the good believers might be spared.

The prophet worm was put in a jar at the highest point of the fort, so suppliants might come to thank Earthworm Sally for her magnanimous offer to spare their worthless lives. Tears were shed, and many vain prayers offered in hopes of sparing unbelieving family members, or bringing about the swift and painful death of other, less cherished family members. High Priest Leo only shook his head, knowing the futility of such petitions. If a person did not commit himself or herself in person at the sacred shrine to the great under-beast, this person was a nonbeliever. And in the final reckoning, no nonbeliever would escape Earthworm Sally's wrath.

At the behest of the High Priest, interpreting the impregnable will of Earthworm Sally herself, large quantities of worms were unearthed from all over the recess field to be honored in the shrine. The Archdeacon and his team of subordinate deacons measured each worm and categorized them by length. The longer were more important and hence more sacred. The High Priest explained that when Earthworm Sally emerged, her length would not be measured in mere inches, nor even in feet, but in miles.

On Friday during second break, High Priest Leo had

just completed a special ritual with the prophet worm. He held the jar aloft as he concluded his sermon, while two dozen faithful fifth graders lay prostrate around the fort at his feet, chanting in a low monotone: "Earthworm Sally… Earthworm Sally…Earthworm Sally…"

"…and when the Great One rises from the depths," the High Priest intoned, "she shall rear her blind head so high the sun shall be blocked as if with black cloud, and she shall roar. Her mouth filled with row upon row of sharpened teeth will gnash to bloody bits the limbs of any who dare defy her. She will heave her sacred bulk across the land, leveling mountains with a flick of her head, pummeling skyscrapers with a twist of her tail. Cities of man shall be pulverized into dust and rubble. Crowds will scream and run in terror, slipping in pools of blood. Mothers will clutch their young and sob, beg for mercy, but to no avail. They shall not be spared. None will oppose the Great One on the day of doom, none will stand—"

"I will."

The High Priest caught himself. A murmur passed through the worshippers, as they turned to see who might dare interrupt this holy ritual with such heinous blasphemy. Unsurprisingly, it was Greg.

"Shut up, Greg," said Archdeacon Timmy, "you don't know what you're talking about."

"You guys are idiots. You're literally worshipping a dumb worm."

"Well then go play somewhere else and leave us alone."

"Silence!" High Priest Leo thundered, and the archdeacon returned to his prostrate position. Greg was unimpressed. He remained at the edge of the circle of sticks created by the outer wall of the fort, with his hands in his pockets.

"This fool hath dared interrupt our ritual," the High Priest droned on, "and the Great One shall punish him accordingly. Fret not, Archdeacon, but it is not now in our power to enact vengeance. That would mean mistrust in our Great Protector. This unbelieving scum will be dealt with on the day of doom."

The worshippers picked up the chant of "unbelieving scum" and "day of doom."

"I'm not afraid of any 'day of doom,'" said Greg loudly, "because all this is some made up dumb story. Leo found a big worm in a pile of dirt. Big whoop. I've found worms like twice as big before."

"He blasphemes the prophet worm!" screamed one of the temple slaves, a young pugnacious worshipper by the name of Jake. "We must punish him!"

Cries of assent rose from the crowd. The High Priest lifted his palm.

"What is this madness? Hold your tongue, temple slave, lest the Great One question your belief. The flimsy words of the unbelieving scum should not trouble your ears, which have feasted on the blessed words of the Great One. This scum is but a tiny insect, struggling against of a tidal wave of destruction. Do not listen. Rather pity this tiny insect. This ugly insect, with an annoying voice, who can never understand deep and complex truths, because his brain is smaller than a fly's…"

As the High Priest continued to speak louder and louder, so did Greg:

"Are you guys seriously listening to this? Leo actually thinks a big worm's gonna pop out of the ground and blow up the world? This is the stupidest load of—"

"High Priest!" shouted the same temple slave, "I wish to punch the nonbeliever! Help my unbelief!"

"Your unbelief cannot be helped," said the High Priest sadly, "but I shall show you how the Great One deals with such unbelieving scum. It is yet before the day of doom; she is merciful. We must give the ugly, loud-mouthed, tiny-brained insect an opportunity for redemption."

There was a hush of awe from the worshippers, as the High Priest walked down amongst them bearing the jar that held the prophet worm.

"But is it safe?" whispered the Archdeacon.

"We shall be protected by the Great One herself," the High Priest said, "for she looks up upon us, and sees all."

"It's a worm," said Greg. "It can't see anything."

"Oh ugly unbelieving scum!" cried the High Priest, now standing at the edge of the fort, extending the jar before him. "Cast thou puny eyes upon something so much greater than thyself! Behold the prophet worm, sent in the infinite mercy of—"

Greg didn't hear exactly who had sent the prophet worm, and why, because at that moment he smacked the jar out of Leo's hands. It flew through the air and smashed against a rock ten feet away. The worshippers gasped. One of the temple slaves cried out in agony. Another one screamed that the end was near.

But Greg was far from nearing the end. He was sick of all this talk of worms and Leo's self-importance. He also did not like being called ugly, tiny-brained, or scum. So he marched over to where the jar had struck and separated the dirt with his foot to find the worm, which now extended and wriggled.

"It lives!" exclaimed the Archdeacon, to a chorus of cheers from the temple slaves.

"The Great One hath protected it," said the High Priest wisely.

"Oh yeah?" said Greg, "Can the great one protect it from this?"

He stomped on the prophet worm multiple times. Then he ground the bottom of his shoe back and forth over the rock, leaving only a grayish smear where the worm had once been. Then he laughed, loudly, and stomped away.

This was a time of turmoil for the believers. They looked to the High Priest to explain this horrific calamity, but he retired into the temple's inner chamber and would not be disturbed. The temple slaves, led by Jake, begged to be able to pursue Greg and enact retribution. But the High Priest did not respond. The Archdeacon turned all from the door, saying their leader was clearly consulting with the will of the Great One herself. Finally, just before break was over, the High Priest reemerged.

"Bring that rock within the temple," he ordered; "the Great One deems that it must still be honored."

"And Greg? What does Earthworm Sally want us to do to Greg?"

"Nothing," said the High Priest, despite audible groans from the worshippers. "She wishes to deal with the evil one herself. No one lays a finger upon him, on pain of death. He shall be reserved for her alone."

"Aw, come on," said a temple slave. "Lame."

"This stinks," said another.

"What's the point of Earthworm Sally if we just let stuff like that happen?"

"You may lose belief," said the High Priest quietly, "but that is playing into the evil one's hands. At such times we must turn even more fervently to our great protector."

The Archdeacon heartily agreed, as did a small group of worshippers who had been devoted to Earthworm Sally from the beginning. Such faith was not shared by the majority of the believers, who left grumbling and complaining that Earthworm Sally was indeed lame. The High Priest was greatly saddened by their departure, because of the loss of so many good souls to doom and destruction, and also because he now had to carry the large rock into the temple with only the help of the Archdeacon and the remaining three slaves. They placed the rock where the jar had once stood and looked down with hopeful faces to the dirt at their feet, thinking of when they should all be vindicated, on the day of doom.

But no one, not even the High Priest himself, could've

guessed how soon that day of doom would come.

At morning break on Monday, Archdeacon Timmy made a colossal discovery. He then sprinted to the field, where High Priest Leo was in line for kickball, having forgotten about Earthworm Sally over the weekend. But after the Archdeacon's urgent summons, they ran for the temple.

Or what was left of it. The boys stood on the edge of the jumble of sticks, no longer even closely resembling a wall, and gaped at the scene below them.

"Archdeacon Timmy," Leo said when he had regained his voice, "summon the believers. And bid the slaves to bring me Greg."

All this was done quickly and a great stir had taken the recess field. Kickball was forgotten. As news of the Archdeacon's discovery spread, the worshippers flocked back to their temple; numbers now tripled what they had been on Friday. Jake, the once-again faithful slave, led the hunt for Greg. They dragged him to the temple, where the High Priest waited.

Greg froze. He stopped resisting capture. His mouth opened as he saw, where the temple had stood just two days earlier, a giant, cylindrical hole. Heaps of fresh dirt surrounded its circular opening, smooth on all sides as if shaped by some otherworldly power. It descended so deep into the ground that none could see its bottom, only darkness.

Earthworm Sally had come. And there was now no doubt in Greg's mind that she would soon return.

"Now is the time for repentance," thundered the High Priest; "bring forth the soiled one!"

The slaves pushed Greg forward. He fell, shaking, to his knees.

"Behold!" the High Priest continued, "Earthworm Sally has emerged in the night, and she makes ready her path for destruction. The day of doom is upon us! And she is hungry!"

There were anxious mutterings among the crowd. Some, perhaps those who had not remained faithful last Friday, appeared uneasy.

"When Earthworm Sally comes," said Porge, "she's not going to eat us, right? Because we believed."

"Only you can tell whether or not you have believed," said the High Priest.

"I totally believed," said Porge to the worshippers around him. "Like one hundred percent believed."

"We must bring her offerings!" the High Priest cried out. "Any food we have must be sent to the depths of her sacred lair, to show our faith, and that we eagerly await her arrival on the surface!"

A great cheer went up as crowds of worshipers returned to their backpacks, where lunch boxes and snack bags were ransacked. Mushy sandwiches, celery sticks, granola bars, and clementines were among the cornucopia of offerings that were poured into the portal to Earthworm Sally's subterranean domain, as the High Priest and Archdeacon supervised. Many temple slaves lingered at the edge to watch their paltry offerings disappear into the darkness beneath the earth, with no little sense of awe. When the food tribute had been given, the High Priest called forth a council.

"Now we must deal with the evil one: he who hath brought about this premature day of doom."

Greg still knelt in place, staring into the hole.

"It was in the Great One's infinite mercy," the High Priest explained, "to establish a temple upon this spot, led by faith inspired by the prophet worm, from which the entire world might one day be converted. But then the prophet worm was desecrated. The believers were corrupted. Thus hath the day of doom been brought upon us, earlier than expected."

"What does this mean for us believers?" asked Porge, new to the cult, and still not yet knowing that lowly slaves were not to interrupt the High Priest as he divulged the will of the Great One.

"It means, underling, that we believers shall be saved and none others will be spared. We have no time to convert the masses. Your families. Your friends. Your pets. All who are not with us today, they shall die. Very painful deaths. And who do we have to thank for this?"

The High Priest looked at Greg. The worshippers booed loudly. The injustice of it all was staggering. Why should everyone, the entire world, suffer for one boy's transgression?

"I have meditated on this," continued the High Priest in a low voice, hardly above a whisper, as the worshippers crowded closer, "and the Great One hath inspired me with her will. In her mercy, she hath said this: if the evil one were to repent and go to her, she shall again postpone the day of doom."

In the hushed silence that followed, Greg stood. A single tear was on one cheek, but his voice did not waver.

"Okay, I'll do it," he said, "for the good of the world."

A smattering of applause followed this statement. The High Priest nodded.

"Repeat after me," he said; "I was a fool."

"I was a fool."

"I am willing to pay the price for being a fool."

"I am willing to pay the price for being a fool."

"And so, next break, before the eyes of the faithful, I shall descend into the womb of the earth where I shall offer myself as a sacrifice to the most powerful, and merciful, Earthworm Sally."

Greg repeated this, now fighting back a sob. He would never see his family again. But maybe, maybe they would hear of his great sacrifice.

"It hath been decided," said the High Priest. "Now, to pledge your loyalty forever, eat this worm."

"What?"

"Eat it. Now."

"No, but, wouldn't that offend Earthworm Sally?"

"The Great One commands it!"

A chant of "Eat the worm!" was taken up by the worshippers, until Greg shut his eyes and obeyed. A great cheer followed this, then class was called. No one could wait for next break.

Following the orders of the High Priest, Greg rubbed dirt in his hair and crawled up to the edge of the hole on his knees. The chanting of "Earthworm Sally!" and "Sacrifice!" rose to great shouts, and, throwing up his arms and cursing his earlier stupidity, Greg leaned over and toppled in.

Later that afternoon, Mr L received a call from the head of a construction crew that was installing the new above-ground power line on the other side of the recess field. Apparently, when they returned after school to finish the work they'd started over the weekend, they found a dirty boy at the bottom of their hole. They quickly sent down a ladder to help him out, and found him ecstatic, as if in the throes of some religious revelation. He brushed sandwich crumbs and clementine peels off himself and embraced the workers as he sobbed, talking as though some great miracle had occurred, and thanking the Great One for sparing his life. Before they could ask any questions, he'd run off in the direction of the parking lot.

The head of the construction crew said the boy was lucky that one of the workers heard chewing and crinkling plastic from the bottom of the pit, or else they wouldn't have known anyone was down there. They were about to begin pouring the cement. He advised Mr L to make sure his students did *not* play near active construction sites. Mr L apologized and promised he would pass along the message.

For the remainder of the school year, long after others

had tired of the cult and moved on, there was no more fervent worshipper at the Memorial to the Mercy of Earthworm Sally than Greg himself. Every day he led small services of thanksgiving at the newly installed power pole. Mr L could never understand why there was a small, freshly caught pile of worms at the bottom of the pole each day after school. And no one was more pleased about this than the High Priest Leo.

12

CLASS PRESIDENT

Every November, Mr L's class elected a president. This president's main duty was to sit at a table with the school's principal once a month and listen to news about the school, then report this news back to the class. That was the president's main duty, and also the extent of his duties. Thus it was for all intents and purposes a ceremonial role.

Mr L announced the election for class president with excitement, hoping to drum up a healthy dose of political activism in his somewhat apathetic students. It was a dreary Wednesday, post Halloween, with Thanksgiving break still weeks away. Class morale was low. Mr L explained that the president must be nominated, then of all those nominated there would be a vote, and the student with the most votes would have the honor of representing the entire class at the monthly meeting with the principal.

Albert gave a loud snore. Mr L poked him awake. Porge was quietly picking his nose. Leo and Timmy were flicking a paper triangle back and forth between them. Jeffrey was flipping through notecards, mumbling about spelling.

"Okay," Mr L said, "I see you are all very interested in the rich tradition of democracy in our country, so we'll get right to the nominations. Who would like to nominate a presidential candidate?"

Jake raised his hand.

"Yes, Jake?" Mr L was surprised. He hadn't expected Jake to be so forthright.

"Mr L, can I go to the bathroom?"

"No. We are in the middle of an important—"

"Okay, can I go after?"

"Yes. Any nominations?"

Porge raised his hand, as well as Charlie. Mr L expected Charlie, but not Porge.

"Yes, Porge?"

"Can I go to the bathroom after Jake goes?"

"No. No one else uses the bathroom." Mr L fought back a sigh. "Yes, Charlie? A nomination?"

"Yes, sir. I nominate myself."

"Okay," said Mr L, and he wrote Charlie's name on the board.

"Can you even nominate yourself?" said Greg loudly. "That's lame."

"Yes, apparently you can," said Mr L. "Now would you like to nominate someone, Greg?" Greg was silent. "Not

114

even yourself?" Greg remained silent. Mr L looked around the room. No one raised a hand. In fact, Jake was glaring at people to make sure they wouldn't raise their hand, so this could end and he could use the bathroom. Mr L sighed again.

He was about to give up and declare Charlie the uncontested winner, when he had a sudden idea. He couldn't in good conscience, as the teacher of these bright young minds, just submit to the political apathy of the rising generation. Maybe election results weren't as entertaining as the latest YouTube video, but they were far more important. Mr L decided he would not let this slide. He would inspire his class to action.

"Before we proceed with the voting," he said, "there's one thing I forgot to mention. The position of class president comes with special power."

"You mean like a superpower?" said Jeffrey.

"Sure, Jeffrey, you can think of it like that. The president gets to choose one new classroom law, which he announces when he runs for president, and if he gets voted in, his proposed law becomes real."

A pause followed Mr L's last word, as the students digested this new information.

"Wait, like everyone has to follow that law?" asked Jake, forgetting the bathroom.

"Yes," Mr L said, noting the palpable energy shift in the room. All eyes were focused on him. Six hands went straight up in the air.

"Even the teacher?" said Albert. "The teacher has to

follow the new law?"

Mr L hesitated. But the students were so earnest, so engaged, that against his better judgement he conceded.

"Yes Albert, the law binds the teacher, too." Four more hands shot up. "But I will warn you," Mr L hastily added, sensing something like hunger in the boys that now hung on his every word, "the teacher has the right to veto any proposed law, when it is proposed. If I veto your law, then your candidacy for president ends right there."

There was a smattering of discussion as Mr L checked the clock.

"It's time for morning break," he announced. "I suggest you prepare your proposals if you want to run for president. When we return, Charlie, our first candidate, will tell us his idea for a new classroom law. Of course these laws will support our rich environment of exploration and learning…"

This last sentence was lost in the students' loud and excited discussion as they piled out the door. Mr L smiled. He knew they would be talking of little else besides the election that break. And in fact, he was correct. It was one of those rare teaching moments when he truly felt that he had done well.

"My law," said Charlie in front of the class next period, "is about homework. I've noticed that many students in the class are not turning in their assignments on time. Not only that, but some assignments go completely unfinished. This is unfair to the students who diligently do their work on time, but it is also unfair to the students who miss their work, because they are missing out on the joys of education."

Charlie had lost his audience after the second sentence. But, luckily for him, most of them thought about their own laws and just patiently waited for him to stop talking. That is, until his closing statement.

"And that is why," he finished, "if I were elected class president, there would be strict consequences for every missed assignment. No homework means no break! A punishment every time work is late and—"

Mr L had to stand up at the front of the class to quiet the screaming that ensued. There was banging on desks, pencils were thrown at the board, Charlie ducked back to his seat very red in the face.

"Okay," Mr L said, now with the tiniest shred of doubt that maybe this wasn't the best idea. "Who's next?"

Greg came to the front of the class.

"Hello, fellow students," he said, staring straight at the back corner of the classroom, his hands clasped behind his back. "If I were elected your president, my law would be this. Every person in the classroom would have to call me 'President Greg', and bow like this. If someone, including the teacher, forgets to call me 'President Greg' and bow, he would have to copy twenty-five times 'I will respect the president.'"

"Vetoed," said Mr L said. Greg resumed his seat. Next up was Timmy.

"If I were president," he said, "then I would make every Friday, Friday Fun Day."

There was a smattering of applause.

"I nominate Timmy!" someone in the back said, to more clapping.

Timmy bowed and began walking back to his seat.

"Wait," said Mr L, "Timmy, before you sit down, can you tell us a little more about Friday Fun Day?"

"Sure," said Timmy, "on Friday Fun Day, there will be no work. Because it is a fun day. We can all bring video games or fun things into class, and we will play them together. We can also dress in funny clothes, with wigs and stuff, and bring pets too, like my dog Rover. Of course it's still a school day, so we will not miss lunch or our two breaks."

This clarification of Timmy's platform was received with rapturous applause. Timmy was the immediate front-runner, until Mr L stood up again.

"I'm sorry but that's not a practical law, Timmy," he said. "It's been vetoed."

That was the first time during the election that Mr L received "boos" after an announcement. Unfortunately for him, it was not to be the last.

"Okay, who's next?" he said, trying to change the subject. He picked Jeffrey.

"If I were elected class president," Jeffrey said, "my law would focus on something that is crucially important to me and my fellow voters, and indeed our peace and wellbeing in this classroom. I am speaking, of course, about pencils. You see, the opening at the back of our desks does not prevent the occasional pencil from rolling onto the floor. This is an unfortunate reality of classroom life. It pains me to say this, but other students have come to believe that a pencil on the floor is a free pencil. They pick these pencils up, use them, and put them in their own desks. Fellow students, this is a shameful act of pencil theft. If I am to be president, such theft will not be tolerated!"

He ended his speech with his fist raised high in the air. Reception was divided among the students. Some applauded loudly while others, presumably those who thrived on unclaimed floor pencils, sulked and exchanged glances. Jeffrey's law was not vetoed; his name was written under Charlie's on the board.

"I don't think people should be allowed to call other people names," said Porge next, "especially 'fat.' My law is that anyone who calls someone else a name, no matter what that name is, that person gets spanked."

Porge's law was vetoed.

"If I am elected president," Albert thundered, throwing everything he had into his impassioned speech, "then I will abolish all homework, forever! And every test, and every quiz, and every lecture where we have to take notes, and every worksheet—"

Mr L quickly vetoed this too. That was second time he was booed, and it was even louder than the first. When the chants of "Al-bert," "Al-bert" had died down, it was Jake's turn to propose his law.

"If I am president," he said, "every student will be able to go to the bathroom whenever he wants."

Excited whispers followed this statement as all eyes turned to Mr L. Would this pass the veto? It did not. More boos followed.

"What's the point of this election if everything's vetoed?" Albert wailed. "It's so unfair!"

Students began to rise from desks in protest. Mr L tried to wave them down but no one listened. The boos got louder. Then, all at once, they ceased.

Leo stood in front of the room, on top of a chair. He let his hand fall, now that he had silence. They wanted to hear his law. It was short and to the point:

"My law," he said, "is that the president gets to decide the class jobs."

He walked back to his desk. All heads turned to Mr L. Class jobs were posted every two weeks on the board. They ranged from enviable positions such as "messenger," the student who left class to run errands for Mr L, to less enviable positions such as "bookshelf organizer" or "window cleaner." At the bottom of the list, and usually reserved for a student in some sort of trouble, was "trash picker-upper." The jobs were performed daily after second break.

Mr L understood that if he did not accept this proposal, he might have a riot on his hands. The law did not seem impractical. He shrugged and wrote Leo's name under Jeffrey's. And so the election was set.

"There will now be a debate," Mr L said, "in which each candidate defends his proposed law in front of all the voters."

"Please sir," said Leo earnestly, "can each of the candidates have five minutes of free time to campaign with personal conversations, before the debates begin?"

"Okay fine," Mr L said, not seeing any issue with that. "Five minutes."

Leo immediately gathered a tight group of followers and spoke to them in quick, quiet whispers. Jeffrey noticed this and was unsure of what to do, until Charlie came up to him and offered a truce. It seemed Charlie knew that his law would not make it far in the general vote. Besides, something about the way Leo's followers, especially Albert, now snuck glances at him made him feel that Leo should not be elected. Jeffrey gladly accepted Charlie's help and they walked around gathering the stragglers that were also excluded from Leo's pow-wow.

Mr L watched the intensity of these proceedings with something of a teacher's pride, but also a degree of dread. He couldn't say why, but he worried about the debate.

Charlie was first on the board so he was first to speak. Boos sounded before he stood; Albert had to be restrained from rushing the front of the room. Someone in the back shouted "trash picker-upper!" Charlie asked to give his speech time over to Jeffrey, and Mr L happily allowed it.

"My fellow students," said Jeffrey, pacing the front of the classroom with his left hand in his pocket, and right hand casually waving to express his points. "I am a normal student, just like you. I struggle on my spelling tests, just like you. I hate waking up and coming to school, just like you. I suffer under the tyrannical rule of Mr L, just like—"

"Okay Jeffrey, let's get on with it," Mr L interrupted.

"Let the man speak!" someone shouted from the back.

"Do I have to kick people out of class?" Mr L snapped back. There was silence. "If you get kicked out for being disrespectful, you lose your right to vote. Okay? Jeffrey, go on."

"Some democracy," Albert groaned.

"And just like you," Jeffrey continued, "I have pencils. These pencils are my property, bought with care by my dear mother, and carried to school by the sweat of my own back. They are necessary to perform the tasks of a student, day in and day out, and we all know how hard these tasks can be. And yet, through no fault of my own, these pencils are taken from me! They roll by the force of gravity onto the floor and into the clutching fingers of thieves! Now. All I'm saying is this: if a pencil is found on the floor, it should be returned to its rightful owner. It is not up for grabs. But. If no owner comes forward, the pencil goes to Mr L— for one day. At the end of the day, the finder of that pencil may come to Mr L and ask if it is still unclaimed. If indeed it is unclaimed, the finder gains ownership of said pencil. That, my fellow students, is my humble proposal to uphold justice in our classroom. A vote for Jeffrey is a vote to keep pencils safe."

Jeffrey bowed. He'd clearly put a lot of thought into this. Charlie and a couple students clapped hard. The effect on the audience remained polarizing, however. Then Leo moved to the front of the room.

"Jeffrey has no leadership skills," he said at once, "he can't even spell. In fact he has no skills whatsoever."

"Alright, that's not allowed," Mr L began.

"Permission to respond!" Jeffrey cried.

"Freedom of speech! Let Leo speak!" said Jake.

"Leo, you can only talk about the laws," Mr L said strictly, "any insulting words about your opponent and I will end your speech immediately."

"No problem, Mr L," said Leo, inclining his head, "and I'm sorry if I've offended Jeffrey, who is my classmate and friend. It was merely out of concern for my fellow students, that I felt forced to bring up his complete ineptitude."

Mr L was about to interrupt, but then realized that no one in the class knew what "ineptitude" meant. Jeffrey seemed to smile and take it as a compliment. So in the name of peace, Mr L let it slide.

"Regarding pencils," Leo continued, "this is a subject which I have thought about for a long time. I have researched this extensively, discussed it with many experts as well as average students like yourselves, poured over all the data that I collected, and puzzled over what might be the best solution. I agree with Jeffrey, this is an injustice in our classroom. But we must have realistic expectations. I ask you, classmates, who's fault is it really, when a pencil is left unattended on the floor? Jeffrey claims it is the fault of the desk. That and the power of gravity itself. Jeffrey then asserts that the gracious student who takes time out of his busy day to stoop down and pick up the pencil off the floor, he must then go all the way to Mr L's desk, he must wait for the pencil to go unclaimed, he must attend to the pencil, remember the pencil, then, finally he must come back a whole day later to claim the pencil. The pencil becomes his problem! And who's problem was the pencil, really? If pencils are truly as important as my opponent claims, then surely they are important enough to keep inside your desk. All of us have the same desks. Yet not all of us lose our pencils."

"Permission to respond, sir!" said Jeffrey, standing up.

Mr L wanted to get to the vote, but Leo replied:

"Come on up, Jeffrey. I welcome any response you can give."

"Thank you," said Jeffrey, hustling to the front of the room. He cleared his throat and said, "Fellow students, do not listen to Leo's lies. He doesn't care about pencils. He only cares about changing the class jobs so that he and his friends always have the good jobs."

"Not just my friends," Leo added, addressing the class, "but all who vote for me. You see, Jeffrey wants us all to pick up pencils. If I'm elected, there will be only one student picking trash up off the floor, and if you vote for me, I promise it won't be you."

"That's blackmail!" said Charlie.

"Make the trash picker-upper Charlie!" said Albert.

"A vote for Leo," Leo assured them, "is a vote to make Charlie trash picker-upper."

This was followed by a cheer, but not as big of a cheer as Leo might've expected. It seemed that the class was running the chances in their heads of whether they could afford to risk Leo's favor. Jeffrey noticed this.

"There are only a few good jobs," he pointed out, "and a lot of bad ones. Leo can't give everyone good jobs. Even if you vote for him, he's gonna give you bad jobs. Especially if you're not his friend."

"Everyone is my friend," Leo said with a winning smile.

"Except Charlie," said Jeffrey. "See, if Leo decides he doesn't like you, he's going to make you a window cleaner, or book organizer, while people like Timmy or Jake or Leo himself get to be messenger almost every week. Can we give one man that much power? My law is principled, it is based on justice. Leo's law is a stinking toilet of corruption!"

That's when the yelling broke out. Half the class supported Jeffrey, the other half were die-hard Leo fans. As nothing could be said to sway swing voters, and bribes were not trusted, they quickly resorted to violence. Albert and Timmy were pulling people off Leo. Jeffrey was on his desk screaming about justice. Porge had Charlie in a headlock. Jake tipped desks to spill all the pencils on the floor. Greg somehow found his way to the top of the cubbies and was chanting "USA," "USA," while wildly waving his shirt.

No representative from Mr L's class attended the principal's monthly meetings that year. Pencil theft was still a hotly contested and unresolved issue. The week after the failed election, Leo's name appeared on the job list under the heading "trash picker-upper." Mr L has not attempted democracy since.

13

THE DRUNK

Before the first school day of a new calendar year, the fifth graders waited in line and shivered. The grey January sky had a dull and cheerless light. Winter break was over and none felt inclined to voice his inner dread about the return of school. A rubber ball dribbled against Jake's leg, mis-thrown by a distant third grader. He kicked it.

"You know, at New Years I had like twelve beers," Greg remarked.

"That's impossible," said Porge next to him. "You'd be dead."

"No he wouldn't," Albert chipped in. "He'd just be really drunk."

"Yeah, then die," said Porge. "Because when you have too much drunk then you fall over and die. No, it's not funny, it's true. It happened to my great uncle Tarleton and we went to his funeral, he was all drunk in the coffin, it was gross."

After a long pause, Greg began to giggle. The boys showed no interest and continued to stare at their own breath, reflecting on their present loss of all happiness. Greg began to laugh.

"Got you guys," he said loudly, "because I was joking. I didn't drink actual beer, that's nasty. I had *root* beer. Hah!"

He continued to laugh at his own cleverness. Jake watched him from the corner of his eye. Jake had two New Year's resolutions. The first, inspired by his mother, was to be more positive. The second, inspired by obligatory meetings with school's guidance counselor, was to refrain from teasing. Jake respected both persons— the former considerably more than the latter— and intended to reform his behavior. But, in the silence of that stiff January morning with the threat of a whole week of school ahead— his resolve began to waver. And Greg kept laughing.

"I like beer," Jake said suddenly, "tastes good."

He nudged Porge, who looked over in confusion, then nodded and caught his cue.

"Oh yeah, me too," he said, "definitely. Beer's way better than soda or ice cream."

"I had beer every day this break," said Jake with a casual shrug.

"You mean root beer?" said Greg, no longer laughing.

"Beer mixed with alcohol," said Jake. "I had six six-packs every day. Chugged them."

"No you didn't," Greg snorted. "Your parents would never let you."

"Sure they did," said Jake, then after a pause; "wait, Greg, your parents *don't* let you?"

"Yeah, of course they do, duh," said Greg, trying to recover. "I just don't want to 'cuz it's nasty."

"You mean you don't like the taste of beer?"

"Nope."

"Hear that guys? Greg's never had beer."

Porge and Albert laughed appropriately.

"What? No, that's not what I said, stupid. I said I don't like the taste."

"No way you've had beer then," said Jake. "What's it taste like?"

"Bitter, sort of, um, bubbly."

"Wrong," said Albert confidently.

"Oh yeah, Albert, then you tell me," Greg shot back. "What's beer taste like? Huh?"

Albert hesitated, then said:

"Strawberries."

Greg laughed loudly and looked to the others for support. To his astonishment, they nodded in solemn agreement. Porge said that his parents gave him little bowls of beer as a treat sometimes before he went to bed. Albert added that in Florida— he was tan since break— his grammy drizzled beer on their ice cream all the time, and he'd eaten so much one day that he almost caught drunk and died.

"So your parents don't let you have beer?" Jake asked,

his face open and curious.

"Yes, they do," Greg insisted, then hesitated, caught. "Well, no they don't. But there was this New Years party they had with a bunch of friends and there was a big bucket in the sink full of beer bottles. So when no one was looking, I had one."

"A whole bottle?"

"Yeah. Well, a lot of sips. Like three."

"How'd it taste?" said Porge.

"I mean," Greg had hedged himself in, and now tried to escape. "It was fizzy and stuff, like I said, but I would've had more if I put it on ice cream like Albert's grandma. But yeah. It was good. Pretty good."

"Three sips," Jake said, then reflected. "Are you sure?"

"Positive." Greg nodded vigorously. He had staked his story in its tiny shred of truth and now felt confident in his position. Jake blinked. This was too easy. But boredom must, in one way or another, be appeased.

"Three sips," he said again. "Jeez Greg, that's enough to catch drunk. Did you feel it? You're sure, three whole sips? Did you feel the drunk?"

"Yeah, I felt the drunk a bit," Greg said with a shrug. "Like the floor was in a earthquake and I stumbled like this."

It wasn't until after his demonstration that he noticed the horror on Jake's face.

"But it stopped," he said quickly, "and I was like 'whatever' and went upstairs."

"Greg," Jake said, "do you know that it's illegal to drink

beer?"

"It's dangerous," Porge said, "really dangerous."

"Wait, no, but you guys just said you do it all the time."

"Yeah," Jake eyed Greg as though he were a stranger. "We were joking."

"You think my parents would let me drink beer?" said Porge.

"Or my grammy?" said Albert.

"Porge would be grounded for life if he even sniffed a beer," said Jake.

"We thought you knew."

"Three whole sips?"

"Greg, you could've died!"

"Worse," said Jake, "if the cops find out he'll go to prison."

"Kids don't get put in prison," Greg said, with more confidence than he felt.

"There's always juvie," said Albert darkly. Greg swallowed.

"The thing that worries me," said Jake as he examined Greg's face, "is that he liked it. You know how addicting beer is. Next thing we know, he'll sneak more and catch the drunk for sure. In fact, he might've caught it already."

Jake took a significant step away. The others followed. Greg was standing alone. Then the bell sounded and Mr L appeared; everyone shuffled inside.

Greg was filled with a sense of dread, the burden of his sin. If only he had never touched that bottle! He suppressed a burp and wondered if the drunk was taking control. There was a reason underage drinking was forbidden. Of course there was a reason! Greg resolved to never go against another law in his whole life, short as that may be under the lurking doom of the drunk. As Porge sat in his desk, he caught Greg's eye and giggled, then Jake elbowed him. Greg blinked, suddenly suspicious.

"You guys are jerks," he said.

And that's when class began.

14

THE SPELLING BEE

Thursday afternoon in Mr L's class was shaping up to be a momentous occasion. For the first time since October, Charlie's team was close to losing the spelling bee. And for the first time since Jeffrey was born, his team was close to winning.

Timmy was having an off day. So was Leo. Last night they had been up late, perfecting their blueprints for the secret rocket factory they planned to build at the back of the abandoned lot, so they could travel to the moon. There had been all sorts of logistical issues with Sector Seven, and Leo had insisted on correcting them before they went to bed. Neither had time to even check the spelling words. Therefore Charlie, the third and final member of their team, was responsible for taking them this far, all the way to the final round.

Their opponents, the other three-person team who had made it to the end, were Albert, Jake, and— to everyone's astonishment— Jeffrey. Even Mr L could barely conceal his surprise when Jeffrey spelled "literature" correctly during the lightning round. It wasn't until after the two teams were in the championship that Charlie noticed "literature" was spelled on the class schedule on the board. While this did help reassure Mr L and others that everything in fact was alright in the world, no miraculous event of cosmic magnitude had altered the bounds of the impossible, unfortunately by that point it was too late to change the teams' scores. The discovery did nothing to dampen the enthusiasm of Jeffrey's team as they entered the championship round; the rest of the class was entirely on their side.

Normally, Charlie's team won uncontested. This was the first time in weeks that another team had scored high enough to make it to the championship round and challenge them. But due to Leo and Timmy's lack of even minimal preparation, and Albert and Jake's surprisingly strong showing, the match-up was set.

"Alright, alright," said Mr L, quieting chants of "Jeff-rey," "Jeff-rey," and "down with Charlie", "down with Charlie": "Listen up. We are going to have a fair and even fight. Congratulations to our spellers for making it this far. Each member of the winning team will receive a special pencil."

Jeffrey eyed the silver pencils, which had patterns of multi-colored balloons. He had never allowed himself to dream of holding such a pencil, let alone owning one. To think. He could write with it. Sharpen it. Show it to his parents. Show it to his grandparents. Shove it in Charlie's face. The possibilities were endless.

"Here's how the championship round works," Mr L went on. "Every speller from each team will get a word to spell. If you spell your word correctly, your team gets a point. The team with the most points at the end wins."

"What if the teams have an equal amount of points?" asked Charlie.

"Good question," said Mr L, and he seemed to pause, as if remembering what should happen next. "In the event of a tie, there will be a spelling showdown. Which means that one member from each team is chosen at random to face off with the other team. The first person to spell a word wrong, if the other person spells it correctly, loses."

There was a general clamor as the class speculated about how the tie-breaker might go down. Charlie nodded and seemed satisfied.

"That's so unfair," moaned Albert. "It's gonna be Charlie and we're gonna lose."

"But that is the tiebreaker," said Mr L, "and now it is time for the championship. Charlie, as team captain you will spell first. Your word is 'acupuncture.'"

"A-C-U-P-U-N-C-T-U-R-E," Charlie said confidently, in one breath. "'Acupuncture.'"

The answer in a spelling bee was not considered submitted until the whole word was repeated after the last letter. Then Mr L could give judgement.

"Good job, that is correct," he said, after sneaking a glance down at his spelling sheet to make sure that there was in fact only one C in "acupuncture."

Albert then spelled "gravitational" correctly, though with considerably more effort, and many long pauses, then Leo followed by spelling "justification" without error. Next was Jeffrey.

He stepped forward to riotous applause from the classroom. Mr L may have bought into the crowd's excitement, because he scanned his list and picked out the least difficult word:

"Alright Jeffrey, your word is 'pickle.'"

"What?" Charlie cried out. "How is that fair?"

"Charlie, if you speak out again your team will be disqualified."

After he finished sticking his tongue out at Charlie, Jeffrey turned back to the front of the room.

"Okay," he said, then paused. "Okay, wait, what was the word again?"

"Pickle."

"Okay. Pick-le. Good. Nice. I got this. Real quick, Mr L, could you use it in a sentence?"

Mr L glared at the class, to show that their snickering was not appreciated. Then he answered Jeffrey.

"Would you like a pickle with your sandwich?"

"Oh, okay that kind of pickle," said Jeffrey, nodding. "Okay, now I get it. Wait, real quick, could I have the country of origin please?"

"No."

"Got to be Latin, right?"

"Jeffrey—"

"Germanic?"

"Jeffrey—"

"Okay, but can I just have the first letter?"

"Spell the word."

Jeffrey squinted. His eyes carefully roamed the room. He was thinking very hard about where the word "pickle" might be written. He figured if this spelling bee had been held at a deli, or even a grocery store, he would've been in the clear. But in Mr L's fifth grade classroom, he didn't have much luck. He'd have to rely on sheer, brute talent.

Pickle. Jeffrey shut his eyes. Nothing. Maybe if he tried to sound it out. Nothing. He felt the panic coming. The class stirred in their desks. Charlie exchanged looks with Timmy and Leo. Jeffrey couldn't imagine that letters were associated with sounds at all. It was all too much—

But of course! It was a trick question! "Pickle" couldn't be sounded out because "pickle" wasn't a word that was spelled with letters! Mr L had tried to trick him. Well, not this time, Mr L. He could see around that in a second. Suddenly, everything was crystal clear:

"Seven!" Jeffrey cried out.

Silence in the room. He opened one eye. Mr L was looking oddly at him. Of course he was, he was surprised Jeffrey had found out his trick. Jeffrey smiled and proceeded with confidence:

"Seven- five- B- B-" then he needed a vowel, "U- S- P- twenty-four."

He stopped, looked back at his teammates, and winked. "Pickle."

"Alright, that's incorrect," said Mr L, and Jeffrey shrugged. "Next is Timmy."

The class sat on the edge of their seats. They knew simple math. They knew that if Timmy spelled this word correctly his team would have three points. Then, even if Jake got his word right, Charlie's team would still win.

Mr L knew this too. He also knew it was nearing the time for break. So he threw out an easy one.

"Timmy, your word is 'tournament'."

"T-U-R-N-A-M-E-N-T," said Timmy. "Tournament."

"I'm sorry but that is incorrect," said Mr L with a sigh, and to Timmy's dismay. "You missed one letter. Now Jake, if you spell this correctly, we go to a tie-breaker round."

He looked for a difficult one, as Jake stepped up.

"Your word," said Mr L, "is 'disciplinarian.'"

Jake spelled it. Not only that, but he ended the final repetition of "disciplinarian" with a sweeping bow. Jake was often in trouble, and he had copied out hundreds of sentences with the word "discipline"— about how he should listen to discipline, about how he should improve his self-discipline, and so on. It was easy for him to tack on "-arian" without much thought.

"Okay, that's correct," admitted Mr L, as the crowd cheered. "Each team has two points so it's time for the tiebreaker spelling showdown. I will randomly choose one name from each team."

"I hope it's not me," Jeffrey confided in his teammates.

"I mean, if it was me that'd be cool, but I really hope it's not me."

"I hope it's not you, too," said Albert earnestly.

"Representing the first team in the championship tiebreaker," announced Mr L in a dramatic voice, "will be Charlie!"

Charlie stepped up with a grin, as Leo and Timmy gave furious applause. The rest of the class was silent.

"Well that's over," said Albert. "Might as well go to break."

"Representing team two," Mr L continued, "is—" he checked the slip of paper, "—Jeffrey!"

The class went wild. Jeffrey stepped up and waved, confident that he had at least as much of a chance as Charlie. If audience approval could effect one's knowledge of spelling, this certainly would've been the case. Unfortunately for Jeffrey, it didn't.

Mr L decided to start with Jeffrey. This was probably one the most exciting moments in Jeffrey's entire school career. As Mr L watched him grin widely and continue to wave, he thought he'd give Jeffrey an easy word, one that wasn't even on the list. This way he could get at least one right before Charlie pulverized him and won.

"Okay, Jeffrey," said Mr L. "Your word is 'hat.'"

"Hat?" said Jeffrey in surprise. "Are you sure?"

The crowd banged on their desks in excitement, they had evidently picked up on Mr L's line of thought. Chants of "Spell the word!" died down as Mr L raised a hand for silence. Charlie was frowning with his arms crossed, clearly peeved at the discrepancy in levels of difficulty.

"That's a kindergarten word," he complained.

"We are starting out easier, and building up from there," Mr L explained. "That's how a tiebreaker championship spelling showdown works."

As none of the students had ever experienced a tiebreaker championship spelling showdown, none could contradict him.

"So you're sure," said Jeffrey, "that the word is 'hat'?"

"I'm sure," said Mr L, smiling. Even Albert was smiling. It seemed like, even if for the shortest bit of time, Jeffrey might actually have a chance.

"Okay, um, sorry sir, but could you use it in a sentence?"

"What?"

Mr L's smile disappeared.

"I mean, I know it, I'd just like it in a sentence please."

"The man put on the hat."

"Ohhh okay, that 'hat'. Cool. Yeah. 'Hat'. Can I have the country of origin please?"

"Jeffrey. Spell the word!"

The crowd was silent. A sly grin broke over Charlie's features. Albert covered his face with his hands.

Jeffrey rocked back and forth on the balls of his feet. Mr L had caught him off guard with such a short word. But what letter did it start with?

"Can I have the first letter please?"

"No, absolutely not," Mr L snapped.

"H!" exclaimed Charlie. "The first letter is H!"

"Charlie, that's enough," said Mr L angrily.

"Hehe," Jeffrey chuckled to himself, pleased at Charlie's error; "thanks Charlie."

Miraculously, now that the first letter was in his head, Jeffrey discovered the remaining letters fit into place. He trembled with excitement. He understood exactly how to spell "hat."

"H," he yelled, "A-T!"

The crowd was about to burst into applause, when Mr L silenced them with a wave. The word was not finished until Jeffrey repeated it and submitted his answer. So the crowd remained on the edge of their seats, waiting. Jeffrey opened one eye. They all appeared to want something more. Was there more to "hat" after all? That's when it hit him. Of course Mr L wouldn't give him so short of a word in the tiebreaker championship spelling showdown! That would be preposterous! No, this was another trick. "Hat" was not so short as it seemed.

"Q!" he cried out, "P- R- Seventy-three!"

He threw that last number in for good measure. But the entire class groaned. Albert squealed, "you've got to be kidding!" from behind him. Mr L closed his eyes.

Jeffrey was not stupid. He realized he'd said something wrong.

"No, no just kidding," he said. "No, I meant seventy-*four*! Seventy-four!"

The groans got louder. Charlie was sharing looks with his team as if to say the victory was surely theirs. Jeffrey was on the verge of panic. Where had he gone wrong?

"Is that your answer?" said Mr L in a dull voice, devoid of hope. "Once you repeat the word, Jeffrey, I can say if you're correct."

"No, no sorry sir that's not it. Uh, uh, can I start over? I can? Okay, okay, um, H- A- Y- B- no, no, that's not it. Starting over. Okay? H- seventeen- no no numbers. Stupid Jeffrey! No numbers. Not yet. Those come later."

"Jeffrey," said Mr L. "Spell the word."

"I really want to Mr L, see I've got it in my head but there's a lot of pressure and—"

"Give it your best shot."

"I'm trying sir, really I am, but it's all these numbers and getting the right one—"

"There are no numbers in the word 'hat'! Or in any other word! Just letters! Three letters!"

Now the class was really quiet. The last time they'd heard Mr L yell that loud was when Jake decided to bring in mud pies for his birthday to distribute to the class, instead of cupcakes. Jeffrey understood he was standing on thin ice. But he also wasn't going down without a fight.

"Okay," he said slowly, with the intention of stalling until another spark of sudden genius struck. "Okay. 'Hat.' Three letters. First one is 'H'. Second one… The second one…"

That's when Jeffrey noticed the clock.

"Mr L! Look at the time!"

"I know it's time for break, Jeffrey, but we need to finish this spelling bee."

"No, but it's late and—"

"Jeffrey, this is non-negotiable. Spell 'hat' so Charlie can spell his word and we can be done."

"My mom's supposed to pick me up early because we're going on a weekend trip and we need to go to the airport and catch a—"

"Jeffrey—"

"Plane and she said I had to be all packed up and ready by the *start* of break but I totally forgot because of the spelling—"

"Jeffrey, now's not the time to invent—"

"And she's gonna be so mad if I'm late sorry Mr L maybe we can call it a tie for now and finish the spelling bee later?"

"Jeffrey! Enough! Get back to the front of the room, now!"

Jeffrey had made a desperate scramble to pack his books. With one more glance at the clock, he straightened. Then moved, slowly, back to the board.

"No more wild stories," Mr L said. "You are stalling. If you don't spell the word, your team forfeits."

Jeffrey was not going to let his team down. They'd gotten this far. He couldn't abandon them now.

"But, but," he stuttered.

"No excuses. Spell 'hat.'"

"We're going to miss our—"

"Spell 'hat' right now or I'll give you so much detention you'll miss your entire life!"

Jeffrey's lip quivered. He would not open his mouth and spell the word, because he did not know how to spell the word. But he would not let his team down. A single tear slipped along his left cheek.

"Spell it!" Mr L was saying, "Spell 'hat'! Jeffrey! No more stalling or excuses, spell 'hat'! Spell 'hat'! Spell 'hat'!"

The class watched with open mouths. In later years they would come to understand this as the moment Mr L had a "nervous breakdown." It's an event that happens in most teacher's lives, in some more often than others. But one thing was clear. This was even worse than the mud-pies.

Now Mr L was standing in front of Jeffrey, repeating his command to "Spell HAT!" Jeffrey refused to speak. The class looked on in horror. That's when Jeffrey's mother entered the room, wondering what in the world was holding her son.

Jeffrey's family made it to their flight, but only barely. The spelling bee championship was rescheduled for next Monday, after an extended and heartfelt apology from Mr L for his behavior. Jeffrey had another shot at the tiebreaker round and lost spectacularly when he spelled "dog" with exactly six Fs in a row, among other letters. But for one weekend, that blissful family weekend away, Jeffrey was a spelling champion.

ABOUT THE AUTHOR

Tom Longano was inspired to write his Boy Stories Series after teaching at an all-boys elementary school, where he told countless stories and loved encouraging boys to read. He decided to write down the stories he shared with his students, to help spread a love of reading to a wider audience of boys.

The Boy Stories collections have now been read by thousands of imaginative, crazy boys.

Listen to Tom read the audiobook of *The Blue Book of Stories* on the **Boy Stories Podcast** (available on all platforms), and for more info on all things Boy Stories, check out **www.tomlongano.com**.

THE RED BOOK OF STORIES
— Boy Stories Volume II—

Jeffrey, Albert, Leo, Greg and all the gang return with more crazy antics in Mr L's fifth grade classroom. Fourteen new laugh-out-loud stories with math blasters, kickball, cute kittens, epic fights, scary camping trips, a zombie apocalypse, and so much more…

Available now on Amazon and Tomlongano.com.

Made in the USA
Las Vegas, NV
12 April 2024

88613718R00090